Love And All That

By Sean Harding

ISBN 978-0-9933539-0-1

Dedication

For Steven, beloved son and brother, who enhanced our lives for thirty-four years.

For Audrey. Just for being you.

Our children, Amy, Mark, Ronan and Jill. I'm always completely amazed by you.

My sister, Johanna. I've never known anyone so liked and loved by so many.

My parents, Sean Snr. and June. Your integrity is my legacy.

And Lexi and Grace. Earthbound angels.

Special Thanks

I must mention my English teacher, Class of '76. Tony Gallagher demonstrated that teaching isn't just about conveying the knowledge at hand and hoping it might stick by osmosis, but by invoking a sense of wonderment within our young minds.

Without doubt, room 25 in Navan Vocational School was where my passion for the English language was ignited, and for that, Mr Gallagher, "Sir", I'll always be grateful.

When I first looked at e-publishing, like a lot of people, I knew very little about it. From the moment I met Orla Kelly, this lady couldn't do enough to help me, working tirelessly to get this book online. If you are thinking of going this route, I can highly recommend the services of Orla Kelly Self-Publishing. Orla, a big thanks. New Irish writers need a friend like you.

Sean Harding June 2015

About The Author

Sean Harding lives in Co. Meath, with his wife Audrey and they have four children, a niece and one grandchild. He worked in the steel industry for thirty-four years and enjoys car restoration and aviation. Sean first took up writing back in 2011 and his key influences are Sam Millar and Cormac McCarthy, authors, he say, who can truly make you feel what the character feels.

John Lennon was right.

All you need is love.

But humans are too complex to leave it at that. We dilute love with jealousy, possessiveness, infidelity. How many jurors have heard the words 'I did it for love'?

In these stories I've attempted to explore this inescapable thing we call love and the darker paths it leads us along. Heaven wouldn't work without it. And try naming a song that doesn't mention it.

All you need is love.

If only it was that simple.

Sean Harding June 2015

Table of Contents

THE RIVER

The River

The constant din of the river went on all night. The gush and gurgle of the water was relentless. Laura thought it would drive her mad. Where did it all come from?

She sat on the bank, watching the ebbing water form suds on the weir. In the east, the sun was beginning to fidget from its rest, its first faint sprinklings of light softened by early morning mist.

Laura shivered. She had sat there so long, the numbness was like a paralysis. She looked at the empty vodka bottle in her hand.

"Damn it. Even you've abandoned me."

She tossed it into the river. It made a plunking sound as it hit the water. She watched its neck dip and rise as the rushing current carried it away.

A thousand thoughts bubbled like thick gravy in her head. Only one thought was clear as she watched the bottle finally sink.

"Me next."

But, as the alcohol had worn off, so too had the courage it had given her. The river was less alluring now. It no longer looked like the problem solver it had been hours ago. More thoughts began to rise out of the gloop. Thoughts about what had brought her here.

The distant song of a summer lark rising from its slumber brought her back to younger years. 1978. Seventeen, and her world was new. Wanting to be explored. Tasted and tested. And what sweeter taste than the nectar of love.

Her school friends would dream about David Soul and David Essex, but Laura had David Connor. No bedroom poster, but real and living. Tall and strong, and, at twenty-two he had four years of army service behind him. Hand in hand, they'd walk along this very river bank. Secret walks, stolen during his weekend leave. It was no use bringing him home. She'd done that once. During a tense Sunday evening tea, her mother had studied David with forbidding eyes, her clipped small talk adding to the cold atmosphere. And her father, quizzing and querying. Would he be off to the Lebanon? How many years did he expect to stay in the Army?

"It's not all playing with guns, you know", he told David, "you could get yourself killed."

Stupid man. As if David was a raw recruit. Condescending, that's what it was. And then the awful row after he'd gone home.

"Well, Ma, isn't he lovely? You should see him in his uniform."

"And what about <u>your</u> uniform?"

"What's that supposed to mean?"

Her father got up from the fireside, ranting.

"A school uniform. He's too bloody old for you, that's what your mother means."

"I'm nearly eighteen." The mantra of the minor, looking for independence.

But there was no independence to be had in that house. Laura's eyes glazed over at the memory of that Sunday evening. She might as well have brought home a lad from a seminary.

For four months, she and David would sneak about after dark, meeting in other towns, making plans. They'd abscond. Elope. When she'd turned eighteen, of course. And to hell with the consequences.

In a fulfilling of her father's prophesy, David got sent to the Lebanon that autumn. They wrote and wrote. Letters of unquenchable love. When his tour was over, he'd buy her a ring. Nothing too expensive, not on a soldier's pay. But Laura didn't care. No girl on earth would have a ring like it. Or a man like David.

The letters stopped. Be patient, she reasoned. God only knew what the post was like in places like that. Didn't the army have to move around? Be covert. Wasn't that the word? Soldiers couldn't be doing with writing letters at times like that. But no more letters came. She'd watch the news at night, hoping for reports of what might be happening, her father baffled by her sudden interest in a far flung war. From what she could tell, there were some dodgy moments for peacekeepers in that place. It explained a lot, and she consoled herself that the letters would resume when things settled down.

But the letters didn't resume.

And then, the shock of Laura's life. At eleven Mass on a rainy Sunday in late September. It was the part of the service when Fr. McGettigan read the list of the dead. She expected the usual roll call of busybodies and curtain twitchers who'd passed on during the week. But there was a solemnity to his wizened face, a pause in his words that was unnerving.

"Dear brethren, I received a most distressing phone call at five o'clock this morning. It is with deep regret I have to announce the death of David Connor of Ballycash."

Laura felt her stomach churn. This couldn't be right. Some of the congregation were looking at each other, frowning quizzically, waiting for more information from the pulpit.

"Some of you may have known this young man was serving with the armed forces in Lebanon."

Laura's shriek echoed round the church, her mother and father's shocked faces glaring at her. The information added up, yet still, her brain refused to register it.

"David was tragically killed at about four a.m. our time. His family asked me not to make the announcement until relatives had been informed… Funeral arrangements later. May he rest in peace."

Laura ran from the church screaming, her mother running after her, priest and parishioners watching in shock. Fodder for the chapel yard gossips.

"You hardly knew him", her mother told her in the spills of rain, "didn't you only see him a couple of times."

Laura sobbed and sobbed. What was the point in saying she'd been seeing David all this time? That they were going to marry. Her mother looked like she was foraging for a seed or two of comfort, but could find nothing but chaff.

"Wait in the car. We'll be out after communion."

The sympathy of a cold heart.

The drive home was nothing short of horrendous, Laura in the back swallowing bitter tears, her mother up front reading the parish bulletin. And her father, looking like he wanted to say something, but couldn't. Silence, broken by the wipers slapping back and forth on the windscreen. They stopped at the local shop.

"Get a block of vanilla, and don't forget wafers" her mother said.

Moments later Laura's father returned, ice cream in one hand, Sunday Press in the other. Her mother leafed through the paper, commenting mindlessly on various headlines. Life was carrying on as normal for her parents. The sheer banality of it was too much for Laura.

"Stop the car. Now."

"What?"

She screamed some more until her father hit the brakes. She jumped out into the rain. Into the horrid, squalid world. Her mother called after her. But neither parent emerged from the car. The Hillman Avenger revved up, its engine fading away. Even now, thirty years later, Laura wondered how they could have done that. Left her there. Alone with her grief. Their only daughter, crying into the torrents of rain.

There was only one place to go. The riverbank of those clandestine walks. The riverbank she sat on now. The swelling waters had tempted her that day, too and she cursed herself for resisting its invitation. Instead, she turned and headed back home. That rotten Sunday all those years ago had been the start of a long tortuous circle that ended back where it had started. Here. Today. Just her and the river. Calling her again.

Other birds had joined in the lark's song now. The sun was warming the earth. Consuming the dew, gently prodding the buttercups from their sleep. Could it not be stopped, this daily charade? Why did everything always seem to be just fine with Mother Nature? She was like her own mother, going about as if nothing was wrong.

Laura threw her mind back to that Sunday again. To when she finally came home, soaked with rainwater, yet not feeling it. Her mother throwing her a towel and throwing words with it.

"Get yourself dried."

The days that followed were trance-like. The village was full of talk about David. From the school bus, Laura saw clusters of people go in and out of his house, their cars half blocking the road. She imagined their hushed chatter.

"Isn't it awful, and he so young."

"Had he a girlfriend, do you know?"

It was out of bounds for Laura. David's family had opposed their relationship as much as her own had. On the day of the funeral, long after the mourners had left, she stole into the cemetery at dusk, single rose in her hand. She swapped it for a handful of earth from the grave, putting it into a paper bag.

She would never return.

Those still, chilly autumn evenings gave way to winter. Laura's only real companions were her schoolbooks. It was easier to study for next summer's exams than communicate with her family. She didn't ask her parents for much love, and they didn't go out of their way to give it. Looking back, it was probably the melancholy they couldn't cope with. Months of it. Gnawing grief. Uncounseled and cancerous to the spirit.

Her brother came home from Liverpool that Christmas. The Ma and Da all hugs and handshakes. Probably relieved for the bit of life he brought with him.

"Are you ok?" Lorcan asked in a quiet moment.

"I'm fine."

He could tell something was badly amiss. On Christmas Eve, with the parents gone to Carlow with presents, Laura finally broke down in a damn-burst of tears.

"I'm pregnant, Lorcan."

They stood in that front room looking at each other for several seconds. Finally, Lorcan asked the inevitable.

"Do they know?"

She shook her head.

"I can't tell them."

"I suppose the father has done a runner."

She hung her head.

"You could say that…he's dead."

The Christmas tree lights flashed, her tears glistening in the co-lours.

Lorcan dropped onto a chair, unable to take it all in.

"And his parents?"

"Forget it", she said, "they'd curse me and it."

The lights of a car sprayed through the window, creeping along the wall as it came up the drive.

"They're back. Not a word", she urged him.

A salmon, rising for a fly, made Laura jump, bringing her back to the present. The colours of its scales flashed in the morning sun. Just like the lights on the Christmas tree. And then she was back in the sit-ting room. It was New Year's Day. 1979.

Lorcan was in the back yard, smoking. Laura could still remember the look in his eyes as he made his suggestion.

"Come back to Liverpool with me. For a few days. Before you go back to school."

"Why? It won't change anything."

Then he looked even more serious.

"It might. I mean to say, Laura. You have an option."

She felt confused for a moment, until he said, "Are you far gone?"

"Not three months yet."

Then his meaning dawned on her, crashing into his her head.

"Get rid of it? Is that what you're saying?"

Lorcan nodded, drawing hard on the cigarette.

"I'd pay for it. I have some money put aside."

She felt a pang, deep in her stomach, as if the baby had sensed the conversation, and had thrown up inside her.

"Would you two ever come in or close the door. You're letting all the bloody heat out."

They looked at their father standing by the door, unable to answer him. He slammed it shut.

"Happy New Year to you, too", Lorcan said, "I remember why I went away, now."

Laura shivered. He threw his jacket round her shoulders.

"Think what they'll be like when you tell them. You've just seen what he's like over a bit of heat escaping."

Laura knew her options were sparse. In fact, there was only one squalid solution.

Days later, she was looking at the choppy Irish Sea from the deck of the Liverpool ferry. True to his word, Lorcan looked after everything. As far as her parents were concerned, he was taking his sister for a bit of a break. A chance to come out of herself. They were only too glad to let her go.

She came back empty. Empty of David's baby. Empty of feelings, the one connection to David she had left gone forever.

The long wet summer of '79 arrived and she finished her exams, managing top marks in almost everything. At home they begged her to go to college. Instead, she took the first job that came along. Cashier at the local builder's merchants. It was dead end, just like her entire life, but it paid the rent on a dingy flat. Anything to get away from home. And there she stayed, reaching the dizzying heights of office supervisor. Now, so far into her forties, she didn't want to think about it. Life had rushed past, just like the damned river. Only her imaginings of what could have been broke the monotony.

Occasionally, a local would call to the providers. A carpenter, late twenties or thirty. Tall and strong. For a glorious moment, she'd pretend he was the son she'd never had. That she'd see him later. His diner would be on the table. And was he bringing the girlfriend for tea on Sunday? Never once did Laura entertain the notion that she might have been carrying a girl on that fateful ferry trip. God forbid, the poor creature, had it been given the chance, might have turned out like her mother.

She looked at her watch. It was gone seven. Was there any point in going in today? It was Friday. Why not ring in sick? She laughed wryly to herself. Wasn't she sick anyway? Anyone who's spent the night like that had to be.

She finally got up, sore and stiff, and began making her way across the field. The distant roar of cars and trucks heading for Dublin filled her ears. The present world, calling her back after another failed attempt at the riverbank. She thought about her counselor. The one she'd finally found the courage to see at forty-two years old. He'd get it out of her anyway. The man could read her like a scanner read barcodes.

"Are you the victim of you history, or the mistress of your destiny?" he'd once asked her. Wise words indeed. And meaningless from someone who gave no impression he'd ever been anyone's victim. Words from the back of a cornflake packet, that's what they were.

Twinges of hunger pricked her stomach. Somehow it was comforting. If her body was functioning, maybe her mind might join in. Her feet were damp from the dewy grass, but the sun was rising. Her face soaked up its warmth. Her shoulders, too. It was going to be a nice day, with or without Laura.

At the gate, a wren chirped and chattered. It sat on the top wrung, staying there as she got closer. A passing car frightened it away.

As she closed the gate, a voice made her jump.

"You're out early, Laura."

She swung round to see Tom Collins standing there, waders done up to his thighs, fishing rod slung over his shoulder.

"Oh, just thought I'd have an early walk, it being so nice and all."

He glanced down at her flimsy, open fronted shoes, trouser legs wet almost to the knees. Embarrassed, she tried to straighten her bedraggled hair without him noticing.

"Are you alright, pet?" he asked.

"Yes, I'm fine. Why wouldn't I be?"

Seeing Laura's discomfort, he said no more.

"Catching breakfast?" she asked.

He smiled.

"I hope so. Are you going on Saturday night?"

"Where?"

"To my uncle's eightieth, of course. Don't tell me you've forgotten."

Laura hadn't, but it was the last place she wanted to go. Old people and their reminiscences.

Tom was smiling again. He smiled with his whole face, the flesh round his eyes crinkling. Tom Collins. Older, but not much different from the school years. Not in her eyes anyway. It had been a close run thing, all those years ago. God knew, he'd asked her out often enough. But he couldn't compete with an older lad. And one in military uniform. And now, here he was. A widower of ten years, out fishing for one.

Tom opened the gate. The wren was back, hovering and warbling.

"Sure I might see you there."

She nodded and smiled. "Sure you might."

"And come better prepared for your next walk", he said, laughing.

And then he was gone, striding over the field, kicking drops of dew ahead of him.

Laura was thinking again. Walking and thinking. It was ok to be happy, wasn't it? Could hell finally be over? Not that easily. But couldn't it be downgraded? Purgatory, perhaps. Not ideal, but a little softer.

She thought of David. Perpetually twenty-two. And then a strange, almost illogical thought. A coincidence, surely, Tom arriving at that moment. Could it be that…David, somehow, from afar, was trying to tell her something? To do what she should have done a long time ago. Move on. Ever doubtful, she needed a sign. Absolution from the self-imposed, endless mourning.

And then, just as the thought was about to evaporate, a minibus. Close to the verge. Swerving. Just slightly. Gently enough to draw Laura's attention. Green, the paint matted. And inside, men, their clothes khaki in colour. It was unmistakable, and as the bus passed, a soldier lifted his head from a newspaper. Young, dark hair showing beneath his cap.

Just like someone she knew a long time ago.

End

MOVING ON

Moving On

Susan gazed out the window of her third-storey apartment at the crisp dusk of an early February evening. The lights of the city twinkled before her like jewels strewn across a carpet. They were coming on later these evenings, and she noticed it. Spring had come, and she was glad, for not only was it a reawakening for the flowers, it was a new beginning for her too.

She swung around to survey the boxes that hadn't yet been unpacked. The scent of newly applied emulsion filled the air. It wasn't exactly the Rose Petal she had asked for, but Susan didn't mind. If anything, it symbolized the fresh veneer she had given to her life. She glanced at her watch. The one he had given her. The one she knew she should have discarded, but hadn't the heart to.

Seven thirty.

"Come on Barbara, what's keeping you?"

No sooner had she said the words, when the doorbell rang. She ran excitedly to the hallway and let her first visitor in.

"God, Babs, I thought you weren't coming."

Barbara was Susan's sister. In her late thirties she was older by some eight years.

"Come here and give me a hug. I need one!" Susan implored.

Barbara duly obliged. Holding her sister close, it wasn't the usual sisterly hug. This was one that said, you're going to be alright, your big sister will look after you.

"So" said Susan, "what do you think?"

Barbara threw off her winter coat and scarf, and scanned the place. It didn't take long. A fleeting glance was all that was needed to take in such miniscule dimensions.

"It's great", she lied.

"Isn't it? The painter will finish the two bedrooms next week. Come and look at the kitchen."

Her sister watched as she pulled open cupboards and drawers, extolling the virtues of flat pack kitchens. It broke her heart to see Susan put such a brave face on her situation. There was nothing really wrong with the place. In fact it was quite nice, despite its size. But it was a far cry from the leafy lanes of suburbia Susan had been used to. Barbara reached into to her bag and pulled out a bottle of wine. She held it aloft like a trophy. Susan laughed softly.

"I'm way ahead of you, sister", she said, "there's one chilling in the fridge already."

"Well c'mon then, what are we waiting for?"

It was dark now. Susan drew the blinds and lit the gas fire, while her sister uncorked the wine. The flames flickered on the walls, and at last there was a cosiness in the room. The sisters ensconced themselves on black leather chairs, only delivered that afternoon.

No words were spoken for a moment. Susan ran her fingers through her subtle blonde hair.

"I was thinking of going auburn. What do you think? Maybe shorten it a little."

Barbara didn't really know how to answer her. She saw it as another way of getting rid of the past. Then she became distracted by something on the table.

"Oh my God, Susan, I thought you'd have thrown that out by now, or even burned it."

Susan looked a little sheepish as her sister pulled an album towards her. She read the gold lettering on the cover aloud.

"The Wedding of David and Susan Brogan, May 14th 2004."
"Well, it was a great day, wasn't it? Didn't we all look well?" Susan said, defensively.

Barbara leafed through the pages. She stopped at a picture of Susan and her new husband coming out of the church.

"Look at him, Babs,"Susan continued, "you can't deny he was a fine thing."

Barbara took a gulp of wine and looked over at her. She worried when Susan said things like that. It made her wonder was there a chance she still might go back to this man. She still had that glazed look in her eyes when she spoke about him. Just sometimes.

Barbara knew she had to be brazen.

"For God's sake, Susan, there you are, arm in arm with him eight years ago. Here you are today in your little flat. Have you forgotten everything in between?"

Susan turned her gaze to the fire. "Don't start, Barbara."

Barbara slammed the album shut. It made Susan jump.

"Let me take this. I'll get rid of it for you."

"NO!"

She said it with such conviction, this avenue was obviously to be avoided. "I'll do it in my own time."

Susan stared pensively into the flames again, her soft features etched with sadness. "I know I've been a fool."

Barbara tried to console her. "We were all fools as far as David Brogan was concerned. Didn't Mother call him the son she never had?"

Susan smiled wryly. "And she on her deathbed, telling him to look after me. Little did she know…" She stopped suddenly.

But Barbara wanted her to continue.

"Go on Susie."

The little smile had vanished.

"Three months. Three months of wedded bliss. I always called that my honeymoon. I can almost pinpoint when it all started. The final. Standing there, in the freezing cold, watching that bloody match. He was going for a goal and the ref blew his whistle. You should have seen it, Babs. I thought Dave was going to hit the guy. It was his eyes. Black with rage."

She hesitated a moment as the memory resurfaced. How her husband had stood there, flaying his arms around wildly, muddied hair stuck to the back of his neck.

"I don't know what he'd done wrong", she continued, "but the ref was having none of it. Out came the red card and off went David."

Barbara could see she had Susan on a little roll.

"How did you feel?" she asked.

"Afraid. For the first time I was afraid of him. The drive home was horrendous. Hardly a word spoken. Just him thumping the steering wheel and cursing that ref. I said the wrong thing, of course. 'It was just a match. There's always next season.' Talk about petrol on a fire. He grabbed my coat with one hand and shook me."

Susan subconsciously placed her hand on her chest and twisted her blouse, as if to mimic his action. Not that Barbara needed a practical demonstration. It was all too easy to imagine.

Susan flicked a speck of dirt off her trousers. It landed on the hearth like a spent meteorite.

"That was the start of it," she said flippantly. "Yeah, just because a fella looks good runnin' round the pitch in shorts, doesn't make him good marriage material."

Barbara knew by her nonchalance she was trying to wrap up the conversation.

"Honest to God, Susie, we all loved him. We hadn't a clue. At least not for a long time."

"Nobody had," Susan sighed, "It was like that damned referee had opened up Pandora's Box that Sunday, and I sure as hell couldn't put the lid back on. Keep your trap shut, Susan, and he'll be fine. Just don't set him off. But anything did. In fact, everything did. The credit card bill, the traffic, burnt toast."

Her voice faltered. Barbara worried she was pressing her too hard. But she was gunning for some sort of result. What exactly, she didn't know. She only knew this conversation had been a long time coming.

Susan looked at the dregs in her glass. "Time to open up yours now, big sister."

Ordinarily, Barbara would have been delighted, but this had inter-rupted the flow. However, it didn't take long for Susan to return with a new bottle and a corkscrew. She sat upright in the chair and gripped the neck of the bottle to uncork it, flicking her hair to one side as she twisted the corkscrew.

Barbara noticed, not for the first time, how pretty she was. With her green eyes and cute, upturned nose, it wouldn't have been hard for her to have gotten noticed by David Brogan. Or Martin O`Connor.

Or Mike Dennehy. All crazy for Susan. But no, it had to be Brogan or nobody.

The cork popped, and wine glugged into their glasses again. Barbara fumbled for the words to resume the chat, but Susan suddenly cut in with a click of her fingers.

"Oh, by the way, I`ll have that five hundred back to you on Thursday. I'm meeting with the solicitor then."

"There's no hurry, really."

More silence. Susan had a solemn look in her eyes.

"Is Dad still mad at me? I don't think he'll ever forgive me for leaving Dave."

Barbara said nothing. Instead, she pulled her bag toward her and took out an envelope.

"He asked me to give you this."

"Oh God. Has he finally disowned me?" she asked, running a thumbnail along the seam.

She peered inside and the raised her eyebrows in surprise. She withdrew a neat bundle of fifty- Euro notes.

"Oh my God, Babs. There must be…what, a grand here?"

"I'd say so. I`d also say you're forgiven, alright. He wants to know when his little girl is coming to see him."

Susan smiled. A smile of relief, knowing her Father had come round.

"You know, Barbara, I think I must have stuck it out for so long just to keep other people happy"

Barbara couldn't argue with that.

"You mean the people who thought David was a great fella. A gentleman." Susan sighed.

"Do you mind if I smoke?"

"Only if I can have one, too."

She wasn't a regular smoker, but it had become a crutch for her recently. A saucer was retrieved from the kitchen to serve as an ashtray. Susan pressed the cigarette to her lips and inhaled. She began to speak again.

"Good old Dad. Do you remember when I couldn't visit home for a fortnight because I had a black eye?"

Barbara hadn't forgotten about that, and the mention of it sickened her. She still had the album on her lap and threw it onto the table as if it had suddenly morphed into a plate of worms.

"Yes, sis. I remember. How many more of those did you have that we didn't know about?"

A tear trickled down Susie's face. It rolled off her chin and dripped into her glass of wine. That tear became the key to a floodgate.

"You'll never know, Babs. No one will ever know." Barbara got up and sat on the arm of her chair and rubbed her back.

"Go on girl. Cry a river." It was all she could think of saying. And Susan did cry. Eight years worth. All in one go. Barbara wanted to cry too. Susan had been strong once. Fiesty. Now she was just a pathetic little creature in her arms. She gripped her tightly, and they swayed back and forth gently, like a mother comforting an injured child. It was best to say nothing for a moment or two. There was another wave of tears. It was too much for Barbara now. She could hold her own tears back no longer. Tears of guilt. Guilty for having known so much and having done so little.

Still, she was here now. If she only did one thing for Susan, it would be to make sure David Brogan never returned to charm her back into his grip again. Divorce papers could be torn in two, the same as a marriage contract. An intelligent woman her sibling may have been, but Barbara knew there was a smouldering ember somewhere in her heart for this man. She aimed to throw cold water on the last little flame until it hissed like a dying serpent. Susan's sobbing finally eased, and Barbara felt she could let her go.

"God, that felt good, Babs."

"I bet it did, it was a long time coming."

Barbara handed her a handkerchief and she dabbed her eyes.

"Why did I keep going back to him?"

"You weren't the first woman to try and keep a bad marriage going."

"My marriage was a mirage," she replied, laughing softly at the witty remark. "Looking back, it was all too whirlwind, wasn't it?"

Barbara wasn't going to start a game of "I told you so". How futile would that be?

"You seemed to know what you were doing at the time."

"But did I? I mean, coming home to your parents after four weeks of courtship with a ring on your finger. That's hardly responsible, is it?"

She rested her chin on her hand. "God, the look in their faces."

"Well," said Barbara, "he did seem to be the one."

"He *was* the one."

She topped up Barbara's glass and dribbled the last few drops into her own.

"I just didn't see it. That I was being railroaded. His insistence on getting married that summer. He couldn't nail me down quickly enough. It was all so fast. Nobody…" She struggled to finish the sentence. Barbara did it for her.

"Nobody shouted stop. Right?"

Susan nodded.

"Would you have stopped, Susie?"

"Honestly? No. You know I wouldn't have. Not for you. Not for Mum or Dad. Not for anybody. Did Cinderella stop for Prince Charming? She married him in the time it took to tell the story. I was no bloody different. And now look at me. Christ Barbara, I'm thirty this year."

"Yeah? So what. You're still young. Still pretty. I'll be forty next year."

Susan smiled.

"And look at you. Still filling your jeans like a teenager. And you're still complaining. Anyway, you have Gerry. He'll always love you, no matter what."

This was true. But it wasn't a night for sibling upmanship. So Barbara quickly moved on.

"At least you're not stuck with a kid or two."

"Oh Barbara, don't say it like it's a good thing. A boy and a girl. That was my dream. But he wasn't going to share me with any child. The selfish pig."

Barbara was shocked. It was the first time she heard Susie being so caustic about her ex-husband. She gave herself a mental thumbs up. This girl was finally seeing the light.

The two women gazed wistfully into the fire again. Their thoughts were interrupted by a short bleep from Barbara's watch.

"God, its twelve, Susie. I should be going....unless you want me to stay?"

"Sure where would I put you? I still only have one bed."

"We could share. Pretend we were kids again."

"No, Babs, I'll be fine. I've got to get used to this, haven't I?"

Barbara could only nod in agreement. Susan began to wave a folded newspaper over her head to disperse the cigarette smoke hanging in the air. Barbara pulled on her coat and flicked her hair over the collar.

"Are you sure you'll be ok?"

"Yes, I promise."

"I love you. You know that, don't you?"

Susan nodded. "I love you, too."

She still had the paper in her hand. A headline caught her eye. 'Better Times Ahead.'

"Would you look at that. Is it an omen, do you think?"

Barbara peered at the page.

"It must be. Look at the reporter's name."

And she read it out.

"Betty Hagen."

Betty, like their mother.

"She always said she'd look after us when she was gone, didn't she?" said Susan.

Barbara slung her bag over her shoulder and looked at her little sister, her arms outstretched. They hugged tightly. Like loving sisters should. Susan felt small and vulnerable in her embrace.

"C'mon, see me to the door."

As Barbara walked onto the landing area, a young man was turning the key in the door of his apartment. He was about Susan's age, maybe a year or two older. Tall with sandy hair, lightly gelled. He wore a black leather jacket, turned up at the collar. As the door gave way, he glanced over at the sisters and flashed a smile, his eyes blue and piercing. With a polite nod of his head, he bid them goodnight. Susan returned the gesture, with a little wave for good measure. As the guy disappeared inside, Barbara looked her sister.

"Don't you think you should give men a break for a while?"

"Just being neighbourly, sis, that's all."

Before Barbara could reply, she dashed back into the living room. She returned and handed her something. It was the wedding album.

"Your right Babs, it has to go."

Barbara snatched it quickly, and left before her sister had time to reconsider.

Susan shut the door. The bolt cut into the silence like an arrow. She went to the window again, lifted the blind, and lit another cigarette.

In the reflection, she saw the remnants of the night's tears glisten in the flame light. Once again, she surveyed the city laid out before her, defined only by a sprinkling of lights. Nothing but lights. Buildings and cars hidden by darkness, their occupants invisible. No troubles or problems. A perfect world. Until dawn would come, spoiling it all. Casting cold, harsh light on everything. And everyone. Making all their troubles visible again.

There had to be scores of women out there trying to hold it together. Men too. Battling whatever odds their hand of cards had dealt them. At least her battle was over. And her war. No victors. Just liberation. That would do for now.

End

TOMB

Tomb

6:27 am

The big white clock on the wall says so. Why did they have to put it there? Over the door. Opposite my bed. Tick, tick, tick. Round it goes, that second hand. A chisel, etching away at time. Of course, they don't know I can tell the hour. Those nurses, they think I'm stupid. Here's Ruby again, shining the torch into my eyes. Writing down the result. The same as yesterday. The same as every bloody day. I'm alive. Just. What more do you need to know?

"Poor oul' divil", she says, "I wonder does he understand a word we're saying?"

Oh, I understand alright, Ruby. Adam understands everything. If you knew that, you'd keep your mouth shut.

"That Miasthenia, isn't it awful, all the same? And he's barely for-ty."

Really, Ruby. You don't say. How about trading places. Let me jump into your body, loathsome as it is. At least it would get me around for a while. Now there's a thought. You down at Mannings bar supping a pint and drawing on a cigarette.

"Look, Mary, I swear there's a smile on his face."

Mary looks at me blankly, then shakes her head.

"It's just facial nerves."

Jesus, would you two ever go home and let the day nurses in.

7:00am

Ruby and Mary are going. They no longer say goodbye to me. Well, what's the point in talking to a rock?

Their replacements are somewhat better, though.

Annie comes over and touches my hand. I can hardly feel it, but the gesture counts for something.

Then there's Sylvia. My inadvertent tormentor, though not in a bad way. But still, she taunts and teases with her wiggles and her wobbles. And her sweet perfume. What is it, now? Chanel? Gucci? I don't care. It could be petrol and it would smell good on you, Sylvie. You've tied your hair up today. I like that. Those Bambi-like eyes look into mine.

"Hey, handsome, how are you today?"

I can only answer with a weak flicker of my eyes. Annie joins in the juvenile chatter.

"Let's give that hair a good brush. You want it to look good for Alison, don't you?"

She then drags the brush backward through my hair as if she is harrowing a field. She stands back and declares I'm looking well. Stupid girl. I've been to funerals where the corpse looked better. At least the deceased remembered to leave the body. Christ, there's a thought.

Suppose I'm dead already and just can't get out of here. Jesus, don't bury me without checking first. I couldn't even scratch the lid.

9:30am

I can hear Alison's footsteps echoing in the corridor. The door swings open. It's her alright. My lovely Alison. Lipstick and rouge. Smiling bravely. What a waste of a good woman. A kiss good morning. A squeeze of my hand. This is now the height of our intimacy. She ruffles my hair. Thank you, darling. Now at least I look like the man you married.

"How are you today, love?" she says. I know she feels stupid asking. Well, wouldn't you if your partner was an empty, motionless shell. She holds up a painting of a man and a woman with a little girl, walking on a beach.

"Sarah did this for you. Isn't it sweet?"

Another flicker of my eyes. It's plain my daughter hasn't accepted my living death. The silences are getting more awkward now. And longer. Alison must be wondering am I ever going to slip away. Can't say I blame her. If I could only get them to switch me off or something. God almighty, you'd put down a dying dog. You'd scrap a bad car. But why does the last gasping breath have to be wrung out of me?

Annie arrives with a bag of white liquid, and breaks the silence with more silly chatter.

"Just going to give Adam his breakfast", she announces.

What have you got there, Annie? The full Irish, is it? No. Another bag, another tube in the nose, another bloody drip-feed. How I wish it was poison.

11:15am

"I have to go now, Adam", Alison tells me, "Sarah will be finishing playschool soon."

Her face is close to mine. I wonder did I tell her enough how much I love her, or how lovely she is. Too late now, anyway. Words just bounce off the outside of my head, and go no further.

A tear falls from her eye and lands on my cheek. I can feel it. It's wetness. It's warmth. Alison, my love, that single, sweet tear makes me feel closer to you than I have ever felt. Even when we made love. A little wave and you are gone. I know now the sweetest gift I can give you is freedom. Soon, Alison, soon.

2:37pm

Tick, tick, tick. That second hand is still swinging round like a damn chisel. The seconds are like splinters of stone. A murderer gets years. Me? I get seconds. Millions of the little bastards. Flying out of that clock like insects and eating me.

What's this now? Something's happening. Oh, it's only the doctor with a group of students. Come in guys, the zoo is open.

"Ah, yes, this is the man I was telling you about. Only the second case of Miasthenia Gravis of my career."

Good for you, Doc. They ooh and they ah like kids on a school tour. That's it, get a good look at my frozen body, why don't you.

5:00pm

It's quiet now. No afternoon visitors. Not till the weekend. Nothing to do but contemplate my incarceration. Hmm. Incarcerate. I-n-c-a-r-c-e-r-a-t-e. There. Not so stupid, am I? How many could spell that without looking it up?

Annie takes my blood pressure. She's just had a cigarette break and I can smell it. What's your brand? Silk Cut? Rothmans? God, if you could just put one to my lips for a few drags, I'd give you the Lotto numbers from Heaven if they ever let me in.

It's dark now. Sylvia hasn't drawn the blinds yet. The first few specks of stars appear. They are the last little pleasure I have left. So far away. Unimaginably so. But the more my body rots, the sharper my mind cruelly becomes. I can cast myself out there. The beads of light become swirling arcs of spinning galaxies. Clouds of gas, red and green. Blue and yellow. Waiting to become something. Perhaps new worlds. Unlike this one, I hope. Nothing matters out there. Like, how my wife and child will survive when I am gone. Are all my taxes paid? Is this stupid bloody disease covered by the insurance?

Yeah, I like it up there. Think I'll stay a while longer.

7:40pm

The day shift is nearly over. Soon the other two will land. With their gossip and their gawping.

"Aw, poor Adam."

Sylvia takes my temperature. The scent of her perfume is gone. In its place is the faint musk of perspiration. It rushes through my nostrils. I am smelling a woman as God and Nature intended. I am on fire. Why must she taunt me so? Must that tunic be so tight? There's a man in here, you know. A married one at that. It's almost laughable. I'm cheating on my wife with another woman and neither of them know. When I sleep tonight, I might dream about you Sylvia. Poor Alison, she need never know. Just you and me, Babe. Forget about that boyfriend of yours. I'm a real man…in my dreams. It's ironic that my name is Adam. Because you must surely be Eve. Damn you and your sweet apple.

9:18pm

The radio is playing in the corner. The D.J.'s inane waffle is driving me mad.

"I've got a text from Rory in Ballinasloe. Says he can't stand Desperate Housewives."

Yeah, mate. You and me both. At least you can tell someone. I swear to God, if she doesn't turn it off, I'll go over there and kick it… except I can't. No matter. I'm getting sleepy anyway. Sleep. My only reprieve.

3:00am

On the dot. And I'm awake. That clock seems farther away than usual. Bloody Hell, I'm up on the ceiling. And I can move. Really move. This is great.

"Hey, nurse. Ruby. Look at me. Can't you hear me?"

Wait a minute. How can I be up here if I'm still in bed? I must be dreaming again.

"Adam. Turn around. Come this way."

"Who said that? Show yourself." God, it's so bright. Why am I not being blinded?

"Adam, keep moving, don't be afraid."

I know that voice. I do, but I haven't heard it for so long.

At last, I see someone. A man. Can't quite make him out. Not with all that mist around him. Wait a minute. It can't be.

"Dad, is that you?"

"Yes, son. Take my hand."

"My God, it is you. But didn't you die in two thousand and…oh. I get it now. I'm dead. I mean, passed over. Or something."

"Not quite, Adam."

"What do you mean, Dad. I'm here, aren't I?"

"Yes, but it's not your time. Not just yet."

"You have to be kidding me, Dad. Haven't I done Hell and Limbo and Purgatory and the whole bloody lot?"

"I know. Even here, a man's heart can break watching his son suffer. But we'll be together soon. I promise."

"Ok, Dad. If you say so. If I can't trust you, who can I trust?"

Already, my new found energy is leaving me. There is an irresistible pull backward. I can see my old body lying on the bed, waiting for me, like a tomb.

"Hey, Doc. What are you doing? Don't rub those things on my chest. I'm not going back in there."

I can only hear one word.

"Clear"

Then a slow rhythmic, bleep-bleep-bleep.

It matches the ticking of the clock.

"He's back", the doctor declares.

"Yes, I'm back alright. And I can still spell Incarcerate."

End

THE CATCH

The Catch

"*A*gin and tonic, Harry. Better make it a double."

It hadn't really been the best of days for Daniel. The new boss was proving irksome, to say the least. In the space of a week, the man had changed the atmosphere of the drawing office from close knit and jovial to divisive and tense.

As the drink arrived, he threw the barman a ten and told him to keep the change. Wiping raindrops from the back of his neck with a napkin, Daniel was glad to be off the grey London streets for a while. Normally, Gatsby's bar was his weekend refuge, but this was his third visit this week, and it was still only Wednesday. Perhaps it was time to look for another job.

The usual assortment of midweek drinkers adorned the premises. A few bankers from the city, giddy from the latest big deal. A tourist or two, nursing a Coke or a red wine. There wasn't much for Daniel to do but contemplate his next move. It can be a lonely occupation, propping a bar in a place like this.

A female voice cut through his thoughts.

"A glass of the house white, barman."

A voice that was youthful in tone, yet the diction mature and confident. Daniel wanted to see how the face compared with the voice, but kept his gaze straight ahead. In London, strangers remained strangers, whether they were on the tube or a wine bar. You didn't stare, just read your paper or found something else to focus on. In this city, people were like atoms that seldom collided.

In the periphery of his vision, he could see her take a slow sip from the glass.

Then she spoke.

"I know its November, but must it rain so much?"

Daniel dared to turn and face her. Nobody had joined her, so he assumed she'd addressed him.

"I know", he said, "terrible, isn't it."

She laughed dryly.

"Depressing is what I'd call it."

She ran her fingers through chestnut hair and smiled. A warm smile. Certainly warmer than could be expected from a bar room stranger. Daniel found himself turning toward her a little more. Enough to see she'd gone through her mid-thirties, and if forty was beckoning, it was going to be good to her.

"Do you work in the city?" she enquired.

He took a gulp of the gin.

"God, no. I can barely look after my own money, let alone anyone else's. Now if you want a house designed, then I'm your man."

"Ah, an architect", she said, seeming impressed.

She settled herself on a bar stool, hitching her narrow skirt slightly so she could cross her legs.

"And yourself", he said, "I don't recall seeing you in here before."

"Oh, just passing through. Down here from Colchester on contract. Legal work."

Daniel laughed. "Top secret, eh?"

She took another sip of wine, keeping her green eyes on his.

"Isn't all legal work secret? And mostly boring too. Anyway, that's not a London accent."

"Stamford."

"That's near Peterborough, isn't it?"

"Yes", he said, "about fifteen or twenty miles."

"By the way, I'm Helen."

"Daniel. Pleased to meet you."

And he meant it. Gatsby's was either a watering hole for the boisterous, or an oasis for the lonely. He'd never chatted to a woman there before. Certainly not one like this.

The barman approached, having spotted their near empty glasses.

"Can I get you anything?"

Daniel looked at his female company.

"What do you say, Helen, another?"

She flashed her eyes and smiled.

"Well, this is a lovely wine, I must say. Go on then."

And so, Harry was dispatched for another round.

"So, how are you liking London?" she wanted to know.

"It's ok, I suppose. After three years, the novelty has long worn off."

She angled herself toward him and delivered another smile.

"Well, you know what they say- tired of London-."

"I know", he said, "tired of life."

The drinks arrived. Helen raised her glass.

"Your good health, Daniel."

"Don't know about that", he laughed, "this is gin, after all. But cheers anyway."

She laughed.

"I like a man with a sense of humor. Too many guys are so uptight these days."

Daniel didn't know what to read from that. Was she coming on to him? Probably not, he decided. She was only stating a simple fact- she liked a laugh that was all.

The cosiness was suddenly interrupted. Two American tourists had presented themselves at the bar. A man and his wife.

"Say, buddy, gimme a shot of bourbon, and a Bloody Mary for the lady."

They wore plastic raincoats, the type a street vendor would sell. They chattered noisily as they draped them over the backs of chairs. Helen looked at Daniel and rolled her eyes with pretend indignation.

"I fancy a smoke", she said, retrieving a packet of cigarettes from her bag. She eyed a box of Silk Cut beside Daniel's drink.

"Care to join me?"

"Good idea", he said, "I was just getting that way."

They stood in the doorway. Daniel produced a lighter and lit her cigarette first. It was dark by now. Another day in London was over. Taxis and buses brought people home, their windows filled with expressionless faces, their tyres squelching through ever increasing puddles. The street lamps illuminated the rain as the breeze drove it into their orange light, making the drops look like sparks.

"I think it's getting worse", said Daniel, "have you far to go?"

"No, no", she said, "just Ealing."

He blew a plume of smoke into the rain.

"Ever think of giving up?" she asked him.

Daniel held up the cigarette and looked at it.

"Some night I'll smoke my last one…but not this night."

She smiled in empathy, and regarded his strong jawline in silhouette against the stray light seeping into the doorway.

"I know what you mean", she said, "I give them up every week."

Daniel looked at her. He liked her smile. Even in this dark, dank doorway, her eyes were aglow with the embers of life. He wondered about her. She was running her fingers through her hair again. No sign of rings. Could a woman like this be unspoken for? Her work would have brought her into some worthwhile circles. Wouldn't some smart-arse lawyer have nailed her down?

They drew on the last of the cigarettes, and consigned them join the other butts strewn around the entrance.

Inside, the Americans had settled down. They studied a soggy map of central London.

"We gotta try Madame Tussauds, Honey," the wife said.

Helen laughed up at Daniel. As they neared the bar, Harry was waiting to dispense more happiness.

"It's my call", she said, "how about one more, Daniel?"

He should have been going, but Gatsby's seldom offered such company. His dark apartment in Harrow could wait a little longer, that much he knew. As if sensing his hesitancy, she argued the rain might have eased while they had another.

"You make a good case", he said, "you must be a good solicitor."

She just smiled and ordered the drinks before hanging her jacket on the backrest of her stool. She enquired where the ladies was. While she was gone, Daniel started into his third gin. Or his fourth, counting the double. The hard edges of the day were softening, the idiot in the office forgotten, at least until tomorrow.

"Say, buddy, your lady friend dropped this."

Daniel swung round. The American held a little square of paper in his hand.

"Oh, thanks. I'll see she gets it", he said, glancing at the object. When she returned, she settled on the school again and surveyed the Americans.

"Wonder what they chose in the end."

"Dunno, they seem happy enough anyway."

She ran a finger round the edge of her glass.

"What about you, Daniel. Are you happy?"

He looked straight at her.

"Well, Helen, you've known me since a quarter to six. What would you say?"

"I'd say you were a man looking for change", she said.

He laughed.

"I've a pocket full of it here."

"Don't be evasive", she said, "you know what I mean."

He considered her observation.

"Who isn't trying to change something, Helen?"

"True. What would you change? Your work?"

"Probably, or at least some of the people there. I can't say I ever met anyone who was truly happy in their work. Even you said you were bored."

She nodded, but seemed more interested in his quandary.

"You don't have to put up with it, you know."

She brushed her hand off his. It was only for a second, but he could feel her warmth. Her softness.

"You don't have to put up with anything you don't want to. Everyone likes a change from time to time…even if it's only a brief escape."

He could only ponder her words. There was meaning in there somewhere. Was it sympathy? Or empathy. Or was it more than that? Enticement?

He gulped down the dregs of his glass.

"This place is beginning to stifle me. Fancy moving on somewhere else?"

"What did you have in mind?

"Let's just get a taxi and see where the mood takes us. This is London after all."

There was no hesitation on her part. Within seconds, her jacket was on and her empty glass joined his on the bar.

Outside, the rain continued to soak the city. Most of the taxis had their hire signs off. They kept walking, waiting for an available cab to appear. He looked down at her. There it was again. That look in her eyes, cutting through the rain. He stopped.

"What is it?" she wanted to know.

"The jig is up, Cathy."

Shock spread across her face.

"Cathy? I'm Helen, remember?"

Daniel remained quiet for a second or two.

"The American guy handed me this when you were in the loo. Said it fell from your jacket when you took it off.

He thrust scrap of paper at her.

"What the hell are you doing with a photograph of me?"

She looked at his picture as pebbles of rain drummed the pavement.

"How do you know my name is Cathy?"

Fire was rising within him. He produced more damning evidence.

"I reckoned if you had my photo, your bag was fair game for a search while you powdered your nose."

He handed the woman her own business card. She looked at it as if seeing it for the first time.

'CATHY CROFT.

PRIVATE INVESTGATOR

SURVEILLANCE AND LEGAL SEARCHES.

PROFFESSIONAL SERVICE.'

Her quarry was right. The jig was well and truly up.

Daniel's face was as grey as the night that was in it.

"Come clean, lady. Why were you following me? Where did you get my picture?"

Her hair was now wet through. She scraped it away from her face before delivering a short answer.

"Sarah"

"Sarah?" he said, "you mean…"

"Yes, Daniel. Sarah…your fiancée."

His face was etched with disbelief.

"Christ. I can see it now. That whole act back there. You're a honey-trap. Isn't that what women like you are called? Sent by her. The bloody bitch."

He walked round in circles, hardly noticing the abrasions of the rain. Trying to come to terms with the swirl of events.

"My God. I can't believe this. I didn't think this was her style."

His eyes narrowed to a frown.

"I bet her mother put her up to this. Just 'cos her old man did the dirty on her she thinks every bloke is the same."

There was no response. Cathy, the woman who was so desirable in Gatsby's now looked bedraggled. Her wet mascara looked like black tears. But there was also composure in her eyes.

"You came this far with me", she said.

"Only to get you out of the wine bar. You wouldn't want this confrontation in there, would you?"

"What if you hadn't found out who I was?"

"My God, you're still gunning for a result. What's the matter, Cathy? Afraid you won't get paid? Look, as far as I'm concerned, you were just a friendly face in a pub. A pretty one, granted.

But that doesn't mean I wanted to jump into bed with you. God damnit, I meet flirty clients every day of the bloody week. I could have done that fling before the wedding thing long ago if I wanted."

He closed his eyes and clasped his soaking hair.

"Sarah, Sarah. I thought you knew me better than that."

Cathy was suddenly short on words. Her jacket had given up trying to fend off the rain. It now looked like a sheet of blotting paper, clinging to the blades of her shoulders. She eyed the open doorway of a newsagent's.

"We should take some shelter."

Her suggestion was met with derision.

"I'm not going any place with you, lady. Tell me, what if I had fallen for all that eye-fluttering. How far were you going to take this fiasco? To a hotel room door. Then tell me you'd changed your mind and leave. Is that how it works?"

There was no answer from Cathy, who seemed only interested in scanning the road for a taxi.

Daniel's anger was stoked by the gin.

"I'll tell you what you are. A hooker without the sex."

She looked as if the words had punched her. His satisfaction was short lived, however. What was the point in taking it out on this woman? He could picture Sarah pacing her flat, chain smoking. Wondering how he was reacting to the trap she'd set.

His thoughts were broken by Cathy sneezing. She'd clearly dressed for the mission, but not for a rainy night in Hounslow. The glow of a taxi's sign emerged from the gloom. Daniel raised his hand and its brakes squealed.

"C'mon. You can have this one."

He opened the door and she dragged herself inside.

"So, what happens now?" she wanted to know.

It was a good question, and the answer came quickly.

"Cathy, you may have done some good tonight."

"Really? How so?"

He opened the window and shut the door, resting his elbows on the ledge.

"For months, my brother has been bending my ear about Sarah. He must have begged me a thousand times not to marry her."

"Why?" said Cathy, "she seems nice enough to me."

He sighed softly.

"She is nice, isn't she? And that's the problem."

"I'm not with you."

"Nice no longer cuts it for me. The spark, the excitement. That seems to have fizzled out. A long time ago. I suppose I didn't notice. But Eddie did. I guess he could see years of silent Sundays and the Antiques Roadshow."

Cathy raised her eyebrows a little.

"I see."

"Oh, don't get me wrong. I haven't exactly been setting her world on fire either."

He laughed to himself.

"You could say Continental Drift has set into our relationship."

He sighed and wiped his forehead with his sleeve.

"Not a great blueprint for marriage, is it?"

Cathy slumped in the seat and closed her eyes.

"Christ, it's a mess. What am I going to tell her?"

"Simple, Cathy. Tell her the engagement's off."

Her eyes shot open.

"Shouldn't you tell her that yourself?

He half smiled.

"No. You're my liberator. You can tell her the incarceration's over. For both of us. We no longer have to go through the motions. Besides, the only thing we had left is gone."

"What was that?"

"Trust, of course. The only reason you're here. If she doesn't trust me, then we're like a car with no steering. God knows where it'll end up. No, she should hear it from you. She is paying you after all."

The driver drummed his fingers on the wheel.

"Meter's ticking, Guv'nor."

Daniel stepped back.

"Goodbye, Cathy. And thanks. Hope your next job goes better."

He laughed again.

"Can't believe you brought your card. And you incognito and all."

She smiled wryly and lifted her hand.

"Where to, Miss?" were the last words he heard. Where indeed, he wondered as the taxi's tail lights slipped into the darkness again. She'd probably lied about Ealing and Colchester, but he didn't care.

He held his hand out. The rain had stopped. The gin was wearing off. The world appeared sharper again. And different.

"Might as well jack in the job while I'm at it", he thought.

End

DYING TO FORGET

Dying To Forget

He sat at the wheel of his car, reading some half- baked fantasy that should never have been published. The dimly lit interior made a lonely reading room against the black, drizzly night. A streetlamp stood brazenly, its light cutting through the windscreen, shadowing the meandering raindrops onto the pages.

A glance at the clock. 11:40.

"Come on, you worthless sod. Where are you?"

Back to the book. The square jawed hero was about to win the girl, the ashes of their old world blown away in the breeze of a dawning day.

A knock on the window. Familiar. Nervous. Three raps in quick succession. The glass was lowered, the whirr of the electric motor breaking the silence.

"What the fuck kept you? I'm here since eleven."

There were no apologies.

"It's Friday night. You're my fifth drop. Did I ever let you down?"

The caller wore a grey tracksuit with patches of dampness that resembled sweat. It hung off his bladelike shoulders as if it was still on the hanger.

"What'll I give you, the usual?"

The driver gripped the wheel until his knuckles paled.

"Of course, the usual. Nothing else does me now."

He tried to look the pathetic scurf of humanity in the eyes, half shrouded by the hood of the tracksuit. Eyes drawn deep into their sockets, betraying a thousand highs and a thousand comedowns peered from beneath a hood.

"Money first."

The face inside the car grimaced.

"Six months of Fridays and you still don't trust me."

His words were wasted, washed into the drizzle. The wallet was opened and two crisp fifties, fresh from the ATM, were handed over. Two virgins sent into a dirty world. The dealer ran a thumbnail over the ridged panels on the notes.

"Can't be too careful."

The prize was proffered. Powder, clean and white, sitting in a clear bag, like it had nothing to be ashamed of.

As the client reached for the drug, the dealer spoke again.

"Do you want something different? Something new."

"Don't know. What's wrong with what you're giving me?"

"Nothin'. But I've got somethin' here with an extra kick. Never had it before."

The man was curious.

"What is it?"

"The usual stuff with somethin' else."

"Like what?"

"How should I know? I'm not a bloody chemist."

Silence for a moment, then, "Ok, I'll take it."

"It's another fifty."

"What?"

"Look, I've got one hit left and a bit for myself. Do you want it or not?"

"It better be worth it."

He handed over another note. The key to a kingdom, passport to paradise, return ticket to the misery of the world. Another transparent bag was handed over. For all either of them knew, it could have been the same as the last one.

"I might have it regular", the seller said through teeth stained with neglect.

The electric motor hummed again and he was left to his own world. The driver watched as he made for an alleyway. He'd brought the goods. The weekly escape. For a moment, he was the square jawed hero, the shrouding hood giving him the holiness of a monk. A street-wise warrior, and yet a fool.

A bell from the better part of town cut in with twelve chimes. Time to go.

He sat a moment, staring at the bag. The last peals of the bell and the patter of the rain on the roof lulled him. He set his purchase on the space by the handbrake and picked up a book of prescriptions. The name on top was his own. Dr. John Millar. A name garnished with a string of letters. But nothing he could prescribe matched what was in that bag. Nothing in the doctor's treasury could offer the same escape. He was still staring at his name in print. It looked good, like a Shake-spearean sonnet, but to him it was nothing more than a lament. A seven year stretch at med-school and for what? A steering wheel with BMW on it. A house on leafy lane. A placated father, long since dead. And at home, a wife, young and beautiful, languishing in his loveless wake.

None of it was her fault. It wasn't even his fault. The medical council had cleared him. It could happen to any doctor. A misdiagno-sis of common symptoms, but that little girl had died. A life cut short in his hands. And mothers don't clear you. Millar couldn't remember when he last treated a child. These days it was the middle aged and the old. How he hated them, always complaining of some meaningless malady. Thank God for those sugar coated pills. The placebo, antidote to hypochondria.

He picked up the concoction again. This was no placebo. The apothecary's magic. It had plied the seas from Columbia just to be with him. Why waste any more time? Do it here. Do it now. He'd have to leave the car. Get a taxi. Fuck it. It's insured.

He tore out a prescription and set it on the armrest. Slipping open the jiffy bag, he set the contents free, spreading it round with trembling fingers. It was ready, raw and naked. Like a woman who'd cast her clothes off. But this was more alluring.

A child's drinking straw was pulled from the glove box. So, this stuff had an extra buzz. God, the anticipation. Like the woman had whispered she'd found a new way of making love and she wanted to try it with him.

He shut off the interior lamp. The street light seeped in, turning the powder a shade of rust. A swoop with the straw and his nostrils were filled. Soon it would descend. That glorious cloud. That all- encompassing orgasm. The haze of freedom. An addict he'd once treated called it a suicide from which you could return. How true.

He gripped the steering wheel as if the car was going to fly. And there it was. The first blurring of the senses.

An almighty slap on the window jolted him from his stupor. Another slap on the glass and then another. He thought it would shatter. It was hard to see through it. What looked like blood was mixed with the raindrops, causing a hazy smear. He dared to lower the window an inch.

It was the dealer, his face and tracksuit soaked deep red.

"Did you take it? Did you take the stuff?"

Millar could only gawp at him, like a child watching his parents argue. Under the hood, the man's eyes rolled wildly.

"Don't take it", he pleaded, "there's somethin' wrong with it."

"But I did. All of it. Look." He held up the empty sachet.

"Jesus Christ, man, help me. I know you're a doctor."

His voice trailed off. He held his bloodied hands out pleadingly, like an image of the Sacred Heart. It was too much for John Millar. What was left of his career would evaporate if he had to explain why he was there. The man finally fell against the side of the car, his hands and face leaving tracks on the bloodstained glass.

The onslaught of the drug was rising within Millar. So too was the need to get away. His head getting groggy, he managed to get the car started. Straining his eyes at the auto shift, he tried to select drive. Everything swirled round him like he was in a washing machine.

And then his turn came. The white cuffs of his shirt turned crimson with the first spluttering cough. His body was desperately trying to reject the foreign invader. The remnants of his doctor's mind told him it was no use. The Reaper stood outside, his thumb on the stopwatch. The drizzle tapped it's percussion on the roof, joined by the burble of the engine. All night it would throb, like the heart of a dark stallion. Waiting to take the square jawed hero to a brighter world.

End

DECEPTIONS

Deceptions

"Get that down ya", said Rob, shoving a glass half filled with vodka in front of Barry. The drink sloshed from side to side, almost spilling onto the bar top.

"Aw, Rob", said Barry, "I've had two already. I'd like to walk out of here, not get thrown onto the pavement."

He took the drink anyway, bidding 'Cheers' to his companion, before swirling the Smirnoff round his mouth. The New York bar was teeming with Friday night revelers, loosening up before hitting the clubs.

Rob stood on the tips of his toes, swiveling round like a periscope.

"There's some bloody talent in this place."

He had to shout above the din of the crowd. Barry leaned against the bar, cradling the glass. He casually scanned the hordes, most of whom were female.

"A bit young for us. By about fifteen years, I'd say."

He glanced at his watch.

"Tom must be getting that client's life story. He usually lands the contract long before this."

Barry had only uttered the words, when they spotted Tom Feeney's six foot two frame shouldering its way through the crowd.

"Would you look at him", said Rob, "checking out every backside as he moves."

"Yeah", said Barry, "and he's even checking out some of the girls, too."

Tom landed at the bar to the spectacle of Barry and Rob laughing at the joke.

"What do you two have to laugh about? I hope you nailed down those contracts."

"I take it from that", said Barry, "that you did. God knows, it took you long enough. We've been here an hour."

He beckoned the girl behind the bar.

"Can you get me a whiskey for this lanky lummux."

She looked perplexed.

"Sorry?"

"Er, a whiskey, please. A double."

"I don't think she appreciates the fineries of Irish humor", Tom said.

"Fuck her", said Barry, "give me an Irish woman any day. Anyway, did you get the bloody contract or not?"

Tom let down some of the whiskey, and then put on a look of

demureness.

"Ah, I might have", he said, eyeing a girl half his age waiting at the bar. She was being ignored by the busy barmaid. He let out a piercing 'Hey'. Drawing the barmaid's attention, he pointed to the girl beside him, indicating she needed serving. The girl gave him a friendly wink, by way of thanks.

"See?" he said to Rob, "I've still got the old magic."

The men just shook their heads, Barry rolling his eyes in disdain.

"You didn't answer the question, Romeo", said Barry, "the old boy will want results, you know."

"Do you know what your trouble is, Barry?" Tom said, smiling," you worry too much. Loosen up a little…anyway, that hard-nosed bitch was soon under my spell."

He pulled an envelope from his pocket.

"Read that."

Barry and Rob poured over the letter. The 'hard-nosed bitch' was a buyer for a retail chain in New York.

"A hundred K?" said Rob.

Tom was looking down his nose into the whiskey, swirling it in the glass like a washing machine.

"And that's a year, boy. A hundred grand a fucking year. As long as we can deliver the goods."

The other two looked at him in disbelief.

"You'd charm the knickers off a nun", said Barry, "old Murphy's goin' to be well pleased with you. We've only managed orders for thirty grand between us. And they're only one-offs."

Tom downed the remains of his glass.

"Ah, you either have it or you don't. Don't feel too bad about it, boys."

A girl of about twenty passed, and Tom looked her over appreciatively.

"That's not a skirt," he said, "it's a bandage."

Rob laughed, like he always did at Feeney's rough humor. Barry, straight faced, emptied his glass.

"Maybe we should get out of here", said Tom, "we're only frustratin' ourselves."

"Isn't it time we were getting back to the hotel anyway," said Barry, "we're flying out in the morning."

"I've a better idea," said Tom.

"What?" said Rob.

Tom nodded toward the exit. "I'll tell you outside, I'm sick of shouting to be heard in here."

Barry gave Rob a little glance. He didn't like it when Tom had

ideas. Especially ones that weren't work related. He often courted po-
tential trouble. And he had the feeling this might one of those times.
Rob just smiled. An I'm-up-for-anything smile.

Outside, the street was quieter. Light rain had set in. Young men
and half -dressed girls rushed toward the doorways of various clubs.

"Well", said Rob, "what's this big idea?"

Tom hunched a little toward him and Barry and lowered his voice.

"I got talkin' to a rep from New York today. Told me about this
great club."

"What sort of club?" asked Barry.

Tom smiled wickedly.

"Not like any club on this street. It's a club with girls."

"Sure all these clubs have girls", said Barry.

Tom was laughing now. "Will you wake up, man? A club with
girls. You know…girls that charge. Do I have to spell it out for you?"

He didn't. Barry's stomach knotted. Tom was ok, as long as his
mind was on the job. But he hated the way he had to turn every trip
into a trail of boozing across whatever city they did business in. In
truth, he hated being in Tom's team. He longed for the old days, when
himself and Ollie Jones were dispatched round Europe to chase contracts. Good old Ollie. A round of golf, and back to the hotel. A nightcap at the bar, then off to bed. It suited Barry just fine.

"And do I have to spell it out for you, you've got wifey back home, probably pickin' the kids up from school as you speak", said Barry.

Tom rolled his eyes.

"Look, never mind Sally. What she doesn't know won't give her a hernia."

"Yeah", said Rob, "would you lighten up. My missus has no interest these days. In fact, she'd be delighted to be off the hook for once."

He turned to Tom.

"Well, where is this place?"

Tom pulled a card out of his wallet. "Yer man gave me this. Said it's by invitation only. If we mention his name, we're in, no problem."

Barry turned up the collar of his coat. "Well, enjoy yourselves, lads. I'm back to the hotel. Promised Kate I'd give her a ring later."

Tom stood up straight again. "Not so fast", he said, "we're all goin'."

"Look", said Barry, "you go if it means so much to you. I'm heading back to the hotel."

"Yeah, and what if you let it slip to Kate what we're up to?"

Barry could feel anger rising within him. There was a look of determination about Tom. He'd done this very thing in London last year, and Barry knew he'd go through with it tonight.

"Believe me, Tom", he said, "the last thing I'll be thinking of is you two getting your end off."

"Don't be so bloody sanctimonious", said Tom, "don't tell me you never wondered what it's like to play ball on another pitch."

"Sure I have. Who hasn't? But the home ground is just fine. Now, why don't you just fuck off and get your thrill."

Tom tilted his head and smiled. It was that sly, false smile he always used on clients before moving in to close a sale. "Ah, come on, Barry. Aren't we a team? Who'd ever know but us? It's only sex."

Barry was about to tell him to go to hell, when the big fellow spoke again.

"I meant to tell you guys, I got into Shortalls."

"Shortalls?" said Rob, "we've been trying for years to get in their door. You're as jammy as they come. How did you manage that?"

Tom's face was beaming in the adulation, his chest puffed out like a peacock on the pull.

"The fella who gave me the card said his firm can't handle more orders from them. They're snowed under. There's a meeting at ten in the morning."

"We'll be heading back to Dublin at ten in the morning", said Barry.

"No, we won't", said Tom, "I cancelled our flights. And I've cut you two in on it. How about that?"

Rob's face lit up. "Christ, we could make a bomb on commissions. You did that for us? A gent, that's what you are. Didn't I always say that, Barry? That Tom was a real gent."

Barry didn't look so elated. He knew exactly what Tom was up to, using this latest revelation as a lever to soften him.

"That's great Tom. Where would old Murphy be without you?"

Tom made no reply. Instead, his hand shot up into the drizzle.

"Taxi."

A yellow cab drew up sharply.

"C'mon", said Tom, "we can talk about how we're goin' to spend the rewards on the way."

Before he could do anything about it, Barry found himself sharing the back seat with Rob, Tom up front reading the address on the card to the driver.

The guy at the wheel grinned.

"First timers?"

Tom nodded. "Is it any good?"

"Well, I'll put it to you like this, they come up from Washington to sample the delights. And God knows, they've got enough of that down there."

Tom's face was positively smarmy now.

"Did you hear that, boys, we are in for a real treat. My treat, by the way. Keep your money in your pockets, lads."

Barry could feel a tide of nausea ebbing in his stomach. The driver threaded the car through the rainy New York streets, steam from vents in the road dancing on the lip of the bonnet.

Eventually, the traffic thinned, as the city's heart yielded to the less congested suburbs. The driver turned into a side street, and swung the Buick round to face a redbrick building. Barry imagined he'd made the same maneuver many times, dropping sex hungry men at this spot.

"Seven-ninety", he told Tom, who threw a ten at him, telling him to keep the change.

The three of them stood in the rain, looking at the place like children about to sneak into an x-rated movie.

"Looks alright, doesn't it? said Rob. Tom laughed.

"Are you here to study architecture, or have some fun?"

A guy in a tuxedo stood at the entrance. His frame was almost as big as the doorway itself. He didn't look particularly friendly and Barry hoped he'd refuse them admission.

"Good evening, gentlemen, are you aware this a members only club?"

Barry's hopes rose. Tom, of course, was ready with the charm.

"Oh, one of your members sent us. Couldn't say enough nice things."

The giant frowned. "Who might that be, sir?"

Tom smiled and looked straight at him.

"John Smith."

A smirk crept onto the doorman's lips.

"Really, sir. John Smith!"

But Tom stood his ground, smiling that cocky smile that irritated Barry so much.

"He thought you might say that, so he said to quote his membership number- 379"

The bouncer still looked incredulous, but knew he had to check it out. Looking like a C.I.A. agent, he spoke into a mic on his lapel. "Check out 379, a John Smith."

Seconds later, he wiggled his earpiece as it brought back information from inside. He suddenly smiled. A different smile this time, it was decidedly friendlier.

"Sorry, gentlemen, had to check it out. People try all sorts of stunts to get in here."

Then he opened the door, gesturing them inside. Barry's stomach did a somersault, and it wasn't through excitement. He wondered by what insanity he had allowed himself to come here. He didn't need to save face with these two. He was his own man. Hadn't Kate told him that was one of the things that attracted her to him? But he knew Tom could be overbearing and obnoxious if you weren't one of the lads. A subtle bully, he had Rob almost like a bell hop, just waiting to go along with whatever move he made next.

"We're in, boys", said Tom, grinning, "didn't I tell you uncle Tom would look after you?"

Barry wanted to tell him to fuck off. Instead, he forced a smile.

The lobby was painted a standard looking cream. Wall lamps with velvet shades threw out soft light. At one end of the room, a painting of a country scene hung by wooden paneled double doors. A brass lamp illuminated the picture, like an artificial sun. The place almost seemed to have an air of respectability. If Barry hadn't known what went on here, he could have mistaken it for an accountant's reception area. Behind a desk, sat a young woman. Pretty, naturally, her auburn hair tucked behind her ears. As if on cue, she smiled as the men approached.

"Hello, gentlemen, we've not seen you here before."

As usual, Tom worked the jaw. "Just visiting. We're here as guests of a member. He couldn't make it tonight."

"That's fine", she said, "but if you wouldn't mind signing the guest register."

Barry took one look at the book that was shoved toward them. "That's it, Feeney, I'm out of here. Sign your own bloody death warrant."

The receptionist looked at him suspiciously. Tom cut in. "Excuse us a moment," he said motioning Barry and Rob aside.

"What the fuck did you bring us here for?" demanded Barry.

"Keep your voice down, will ye", urged Tom, "do you want to get us booted out?"

"Yes, actually", Barry answered, his anger almost volcanic.

"Look", said Tom, "I meant to tell you… it's compulsory for guests to sign in."

Why, Tom?" asked Rob.

Tom cleared his throat, allowing more dodgy information to come through.

"There was a girl strangled by some nutter here a couple of years back. In order to keep in with the police, they agreed to get unknowns like us to sign in. It's no big deal. Just put down Mick Madden or something. They won't know any different."

"You're a gobshite of the highest order, Feeney", Barry told him, hardly noticing as Tom nudged himself and Rob back to the desk.

"No problem", Tom told the girl, picking up the pen.

"Good", she said, smiling, "I'll just need I.D. as verification. Passport, driving license, whatever you have."

Tom's face paled.

"It's just security, guys, that's all," the young woman told them, "it's all confidential."

Feeney began writing, as she examined their passports, his need for sex conquering his judgement.

Barry signed reluctantly, feeling there was something terribly incriminating about leaving his name in a place like this. The hardback ledger looked like it might be owned by the devil one day, passed on for his perusal. And Satan would read out those names to their owners, lined up in the lobby of Hell, their wives looking down from Heaven, laughing.

Satisfied she hadn't admitted three axe murderers, the girl closed the book and smiled again.

"We're quite busy tonight, it being Friday an' all. If you'd like to wait in the bar, you'll be called when some of our girls are free."

"That's fine", said Tom, "we could do with a drink."

"Through more smiles, the receptionist announced all fees were payable in advance. She made it sound like they were enrolling on a college course. Barry almost laughed, but the sickly feeling in his gut wouldn't let him.

"Oh, yes", said Tom, dipping into his pocket, "how much?"

"It's one hundred and fifty dollars for one hour. Each."

Tom flinched slightly as he opened the wallet, fat with dollars and stacked the notes on the counter. He looked at Washington's portrait on the last one.

"Goodbye, George", he quipped, "it's been nice knowing you."

In the bar, Tom continued playing the big fellow, ordering drinks. He flinched again, visibly, when the bartender politely demanded thirty two dollars for a whiskey, vodka, and beer none of them had ever heard of.

"Jesus, Dick Turpin wore a mask", he said, watching the guy make short work of two twenties.

"I'd have settled for a nightcap at the hotel bar," said Barry, rubbing sweating palms on his thighs.

"Relax, will you", said Tom, "told you it was my treat, didn't I? I'll get it back in spades when Shortalls start paying up."

He held up his glass. "Well boys, here's to good living and all that it brings."

Barry joined in his stupid toast, but all he wanted to do was get out of the place. They siphoned on the drinks, none of them having any intention of ordering more. The lounge was quiet, hardly surprising at those prices. Besides, most patrons came for one thing only. Get it over, then get out.

The management seemed to have gone to any lengths give the premises respectability. Classical music seeped at low volume from hidden speakers. Barry recognized the Mozart aria, but it did little to quell his nerves. His heart lurched when a middle aged woman approached.

"I'm Jackie", she announced, "if you'd like to come with me, gentlemen."

She was tall and elegant. Her long black dress and pearls wouldn't have looked out of place at the opera, Barry thought. They downed the drinks, every costly drop, and followed the woman down a short corridor.

She wore her blonde hair up, the parting swept in an arc to one side of her face. Though she was a little older, she reminded Barry of Kate. Just a little. Her slim neckline, and still taut cheeks hinted at a woman who must have stunned many a man in her youth. He wondered had she worked this place back then. Been one of the girls, and now she was a hostess, having worked her way up through the ranks, so to speak. Her dress hung tautly at her hips, which swung with seduction as she walked. Tom looked at her appreciatively and winked at Barry. A stupid, roguish wink, matched with a grin. Barry thought of their wives at home. Tending to meals. Tending to children. Watching stories of infidelity on the soaps, and blissfully ignorant of the betrayal being played out at that very moment.

"Connie tells me you're Irish", said Jackie, "are you guys here for long?"

"Just another day or so", said Barry.

He wondered what she thought of three Irishmen touting for sex. She could probably tell they were married. Didn't it bother her at all? It obviously didn't. Not when fools of men were handing over wads of cash. The woman's small talk petered out as they reached an open area. There, seven or eight young women lounged on couches and recliners, giggling and chatting. They wore bedroom attire. To Barry, the scene resembled a teenager's sleepover. The enormity of what Tom had walked them into hit him. His heart seemed to agree, quickening the beat.

The girls went quiet when they saw Jackie and the new clients she'd brought. Instant smiles broke out, like stars coming out in the evening sky. Tom Feeney was grinning broadly and scratching his head, as if he'd never be able to choose one of these girls, they were all so pretty. Rob had the look of a boy scout who'd wandered into a girl guides' dressing room. Tom gave his shoulder a nudge, jarring him from his trance.

"Ok, girls", said Jackie, "these gentlemen have come all the way from Ireland to see us."

The mention of being Irish seemed to elicit some excitement from among them, though Barry supposed they might have reacted the same way if they'd been from Serbo-Croatia.

Jackie gestured to the trio to sit down. As they did so, the girls sat upright, shoulders back, smiles beaming, split negligées revealing long, bronzed legs. Barry wasn't sure if it was ok to look. Faithful to Kate he may have been, but it didn't mean he never looked at an attractive woman in the street. Not outright staring, just a furtive glance, a quick checkout. Surely, he often reasoned, women did that with men, too. Except they were probably much more discreet about it. Though, occasionally, he'd still catch the odd woman giving him the once over, then looking away sharply as she was caught. Barry delighted in that. It was good for the ego. If nothing else, it meant he still had something going for him. That he still had some 'pullability' left. Here in this place it was different. The girls wanted to be looked at, to be checked out. If only because it meant more dollars on the night's balance sheet. Jackie could see the men were uninitiated.

"You guys take your time now", she drawled, "and choose whichever girl takes your eye."

The girls ramped up the smiling and preening, vying for attention. Selling themselves. How the hell could they do it? Barry wondered. He'd seen these places on T.V. but didn't think they really existed. These girls looked intelligent, looked like they could pull any man. Yet they ended up here, making leering lotharios and sweating rejects feel special. His face must have glazed over in his contemplations. One of the girls spoke to him.

"What's the matter, hun? Feeling a little nervous?"

She looked Latino, though her accent was American. Tom and Rob looked at him and he felt awfully stupid. Like a lad coming of age, there to lose his virginity. Suddenly, everyone was looking at him. Barry felt a wave of heat travel through him. He fixed his eyes on yet another landscape on the wall. Sunburnt fields with olden time farmers arcing sickles through corn. If he could have run into the scene and given them a hand, he would have.

But the girls were well used to shy ones. One of them, a subtle blonde, got up and sat beside him.

"Hey, handsome, why bother choosing?" she said, rubbing Barry's arm. "I reckon you and me will be just fine."

Jackie gave her a delicate, approving smile. The girl was pretty with a slender figure. Barry thought she looked no more than twenty-two or three. Feeney was looking at him again, egging him on with that stupid, leering grin. Barry swallowed hard.

"Sure, why not." He forced a smile and Tom looked pleased. Barry was now implicated, his silence assured. The girl tugged gently on his hand, and he rose involuntarily to his feet.

"I'm Kerry."

She said it without a hint of irony, and Barry laughed inwardly. Maybe the girls changed their names for the foreign clients. Got a bit of a theme going. Tom and Rob looked agog, dismayed that he was actually going to go through with it.

"Go on, ya good thing", Feeney told him in a low voice. Barry felt irritated. Only an Irishman would use that stupid expression, and only a twit like Tom Feeney would use it in a situation like this.

A moment later, he was back on the corridor. Kerry was still holding his hand. Her skin felt soft and warm, the grip light yet firm. Like she really wanted to hold his hand. And maybe even wanted him. Her hair was long, curled at the ends. It bounced majestically, almost magically, as she walked. Like it was alive. Which of course it was, but somehow it seemed to be conscious. Aware of what it was doing. Tempting and teasing a man. Silky and perfumed.

"I'm Barry", he said.

"What part of Ireland are you from?" she asked, "Dublin?"

"I work in Dublin", he said, "but I'm from Carlow."

He said it almost apologetically. What interest would she have in a rural backyard of Ireland?

"Car-low", she said, "is that like Monte Carlo?"

"Jesus,no", said Barry, laughing, "it's just a simple Irish town. With the emphasis on' low'. L-o-w."

He knew she didn't get the joke, even though she was laughing. Like she'd been coached to. Laugh at their jokes, no matter how bad.

The room Kerry took him to was like something from a fine hotel. They certainly don't go for tack, Barry thought, surveying walls that were a calming pale green.

"It's avocado", she said, noticing Barry's interest. "They asked me what I wanted and I chose that. You like it, huh?"

He did like it, for all the wrong reasons. Calming, it may have looked, but it did nothing to soothe his nerves. It was just the colour

Kate would have chosen for their living room.

"It's lovely", he told her, "you have great taste."

"Thanks."

Barry knew she wasn't there to talk about colour charts, and he felt his pulse quicken. His stomach was churning the vodkas he'd consumed. Too many of them, and yet not enough, for the situation was too sobering. Like someone arrested after a big fraud, he wondered how he'd gotten himself into this scenario. This avocado boudoir and its occupier, twenty years his junior, waiting to please him.

Without warning, Kerry tugged the silken belt of her negligee and pushed it off her shoulders. It fell silently about her feet. She was naked, except for a thong, black and scant. Its thin waistband sat high on the curves of her hips.

"So", she invited, "whatcha got in mind? Can't do kissing, I'm afraid. That's the rules, and nothin' too kinky. But I'll show you a good time, promise."

Barry's heart nearly broke through his ribs. His hand reached for his chest, rubbing in a circular motion as if calming the shocked organ. She could see she'd shocked him, yet she held her pose, waiting for his response. Her breasts were high, firm and rounded, the ripened fruit of an orchard waiting to be plundered. Barry had been with Kate since their late teens. There'd never been anyone else, for either of them. He'd never been in the presence of a naked woman other than her. And now, here he was. He could have reached out and cupped those foreign breasts, felt the soft flesh yield beneath his fingertips. Thumbed her nipples, dark and rich, like spring buds. She wouldn't have minded. The look in her green eyes told him she was expecting it. Barry's mind began to sort and file emotions; desire, embarrassment, guilt. God, the guilt. He thought of Kate, and suddenly this girl's desirability was fading. He felt as if he was intruding on Kerry's nudity. He shouldn't have been there and he knew it. She was looking at him expectantly.

"So, baby, what would you like?"

Barry stooped down, picked up the garment, and held it out.

"I'd like you to put his back on."

She looked shocked. Hurt, even.

"What's wrong", she asked, "you wanted one of the other girls? Is that it?"

Barry smiled wryly. He was still holding the gown, and he pushed it toward her.

"Believe me, sweetheart, I don't want any other girl. Who'd pass you over for somebody else?"

"Well…you are", she said, her slim line eyebrows pushing together in confusion.

"Please", Barry said, "put this on."

By now, Kerry was aware of her nudity. She took the negligee and put it on hastily, tying the belt tightly.

"You're not some sort of weirdo, are you? I only have to hit that button by the bed and Johnny will be in here like a shot."

Barry stepped back, holding his hands up.

"You don't need to do that, I promise."

She didn't seem any clearer as to what Barry's intentions were.

"Well, what's the deal here?" she said, "I ain't been stood up before, not like this. Ain't I pretty enough, or what? Cos if you complain about me, they'll be on my case somethin' awful."

She was beginning to make Barry feel nervous. He had visions of this Johnny dragging him out, warning him never to return.

"Listen to me", he said, "for a start, you're probably the prettiest girl in this place. It's just that…well, I never wanted to come here. It was the other two."

The disclosure seemed to put Kerry at ease, if only a little.

"Your friends, you mean?"

Barry laughed. "They're not really friends, more work colleagues. Our boss sent us out here to chase some new business. 'Contacts and contracts', he said. Rob is ok, but that Tom fellow gets on my nerves."

She smiled, like she understood. "He's the tall one, isn't he?"

"How did you know?" asked Barry.

"Dunno", she said, "he just seemed a little too sure of himself, that's all."

She was being diplomatic, Barry could see.

"He's a pain in the arse, that's what he is." he said.

Kerry's smile returned, full beam.

"I love it when you Irish say that."

"What?"

"Arse", she said, "it's so funny."

He laughed again. "Yeah, I suppose it is. Arse, arse, arse."

They were both laughing now, loudly.

"Oh, shit", she said, that's so Goddam funny."

Then, she stopped laughing.

"Why don't you want to do anything?"

The question was sudden, and it cut through the remnants of his laughter like a scythe.

"I'm married", he said, "happily. Bet you don't hear that in here very often."

"Oh you'd be surprised," Kerry said, "some of them talk about their wives like they're Godesses…Godesses in the kitchen, Godesses at parties. Everywhere, except in the bedroom. It seems some women give up on sex after a certain age, like it's wrong or somethin'."

Then, she went quiet for a second, taking in the broadness of his shoulders, the honesty of his eyes, the first shoots of grey silvering his temples.

"I don't think you'd have that problem", she said, "I bet your wife is really into you."

He feigned coyness, whilst inside, he was loving the attention. It was true, he and Kate were still pretty much in love. Very much, in fact, if he thought about it. Sure, there'd be rows. The usual stuff. He'd be spending too much time on the road. She'd be sick of it. He'd make the promises. The ones husbands always make. About spending more time at home. Let someone else at work take some of the load. It would be great for a while, till the cycle began again. But you can't be with someone all those years without getting something right. Kate still looked good, better in fact, and the sex was great, especially now the kids were almost grown and she could relax. But, it was more than that, and Barry knew it. It was the friendship, the connectivity they shared. The rest was no good without that.

"It's our binding agent", he'd once told her, "lose that and we're fucked."

Kerry's soft voice pulled Barry from his thoughts. He was back in the green room again.

"Why didn't you just leave?" she asked him.

"Sorry?"

"Why did you go along with this, if you didn't want to be here?"

Barry sighed. "Saving face. Pathetic, aren't I?"

Kerry gestured to an armchair. "For a hundred and fifty bucks, you might well sit down. That's if you wanna stay."

"Do you mind if I do?" he asked, slumping onto the leather.

"I'd prefer if you did", she said," otherwise Jackie'll wanna know why you left early."

Barry nodded, forcing a little smile.

Then she said, "And no, I don't think you're pathetic. It's that Tom guy, isn't it, honey? My Dad would call him a railroader. You want him to think you went through with this so you'll get a quiet life at work."

Barry nodded again, preferring not to answer her. He'd only have to admit his weakness, that he'd allowed Feeney to bully him, and not for the first time. She seemed to know not to probe any further.

"How 'bout a drink, Barry?"

The churning in his stomach seemed to have subsided, so he asked for another vodka.

"Sure, Honey", she said, grabbing a glass from a cabinet. Kerry was no barmaid. An overgenerous measure glugged noisily from the bottle.

"Better put some tonic water in that", he said, laughing. "Aren't you having something yourself?"

"God, no, Hun, we ain't allowed alcohol when we're on duty."

She said it as if she was a pilot or a doctor. He smiled to himself.

She handed him the drink. Smiling again, she sat on the other chair, curling her legs beneath her, gathering the negligee about her like a sort of blanket.

To Barry, the situation was getting progressively weird. A couple of hours ago, he couldn't have envisaged sitting in a bedroom with a beautiful young woman, and she barely dressed. Killing time, co-conspirators in a charade.

"Perhaps you'd like to put on some clothes," Barry offered.

Kerry was laughing again.

"I've definitely never heard that in here before. It wouldn't be worth it, Honey. We've only half an hour left, and I'm not so sure the next guy would appreciate me looking like I was goin' on a business lunch."

She only meant it in jest, Barry knew that, but he felt stupid, and not for the first time that night. He wondered if she thought he was pious. Some sort of saint, turning her down, using her boudoir as a waiting room. Maybe he was a weirdo after all.

Kerry was holding her hand up, fingers stretched, as she checked the nail varnish. He rattled the ice round the glass.

"Oh, you'd like another?" she asked.

"No, thanks, I think that must have been a treble."

She smiled.

"So", he said, "what does your dad think of you working here?"

He was immediately sorry he asked the question, but the vodka had stoked up his curiosity. To his relief, the question didn't seem to faze her.

"My folks didn't know for a long time, maybe a year. It was easy to hide my secret life, what with me bein' at college down here, an' all. Then, one day, at the end of semester, stupid Kerry had to turn up in a '66 Mustang. Cost me twelve thousand dollars. 'Course, my dad wasn't stupid. Knew full well I didn't get that from waitressin'. He figured I had to be dealing drugs or sellin' myself. So, stupid Kerry thought he'd prefer it if he heard the lesser of two evils."

"So, you told him?" said Barry.

"I did", she said, matter of factly, "there and then. Told him and Mom the jagged truth."

"What did they say?"

For the first time since meeting her, Barry noticed her pretty face was drained by sadness.

"Well", she said, "let me put this way, five minutes later, me and my Mustang were hot tailin' it back the way we came, my bags still packed in the trunk."

"Shit", said Barry, "I'm sorry…I mean…shit."

She looked sadder now.

"Stupid Kerry, huh?" she uttered.

"Hey", said Barry, "stop that, will you? Stop saying you're stupid. I'm sure they'll come round."

"You think?" she said. "Before I'd gone two miles down that road, there came a text on my cellphone. 'Don't come back. Not ever.' That was two years ago. Can you believe that, Barry?" He couldn't. He thought of his daughter back home, just four or five years younger. He couldn't imagine treating her like that, no matter what she'd done.

"What about your mother?" he wanted to know.

Kerry twiddled the belt of her gown, gazing wistfully at a figurine of a ballerina on the coffee table.

"Oh, whatever Dad said, Mom went along with it. Simple as. Once he started bashin' that bible, she knew she was beat."

Barry sucked on his teeth, a sharp tut slipping through his lips.

"Sounds like he's something of a railroader himself."

She chewed on her lip, a barely perceivable nod betraying her reluctant agreement.

"I tried callin' once I thought the storm had passed. Dad answered the phone. Soon as he recognized my voice, you know what he said?"

Barry shook his head, his eyes never leaving hers.

"That if he'd stepped on dog shit, it would eventually dry out and fall off his shoe. But me? I'd left a stain on his heart that would never go away."

The last few words clogged her throat, forcing a tear like a miniature spring to ooze from one of her eyes. Wiping it quickly with a fingertip, she shook her head as if to mix up those memories into a fuzz.

"I'm sorry, I shouldn't be tellin' you all this stuff."

She forced a smile. It wasn't like her other smiles, more like a thin, flimsy shield, desperately trying to hold back anguish.

"I've not seen them since. My sister sneaks down here to see how I'm doin'. They'd kill her if they knew."

Barry was searching for words, but he was like a miner without a torch. He wondered if he should go over and comfort her in some way. Rub her shoulder, tell her it was ok. That if she was his daughter, he'd never say such things.

Suddenly, the sound of moaning came from the next room. It permeated the wall. Their ears gravitated toward the sound.

"That's Carla", said Kerry, "she always moans like that when she org-."

She stopped and actually blushed.

Barry laughed.

"Just because we're not having sex doesn't mean I'm a prude. You mean when she orgasms. When she comes…yes?"

Kerry smiled. "Yes."

Then a man's voice could be heard.

"Aw, yeah…yeah, yeah, yeah."

"I think the Beatles are in there", said Barry, cocking his head toward the wall. Then he recognized the voice.

"That's Feeney, I'd swear it is."

Again, 'Yeah, yeah, yeah…yes."

"It's him alright", said Barry, grinning broadly.

Tom sounded like he'd just succeeded in pushing a wardrobe up a stairs.

Barry looked at Kerry and both of them erupted into laughter. Carla's moans we're fading.

"I bet she fakes it most of the time," said Barry.

Kerry looked awkward, not knowing what to say.

"It's ok", he said, it's a trade secret, isn't it? Tom Feeney is in there and he thinks he's a prize stallion. A right stud."

She didn't answer him. The distraction from next door was short lived. She looked like the silt of memories had settled in her head again, bringing a dullness to her eyes. Barry thought it probably would have been easier for her to have had sex with him, than sit here having this conversation.

"So, what are you studying in college?" he asked.

"Physiotherapy and sports injuries", Kerry said, a little smile breaking out on her face.

"Really?" said Barry, "and you called yourself stupid. That's like half way to a doctor, isn't it?"

"Not really", she said, "but there's a lot to it. Every hour I'm not here or at college or sleeping I study."

Barry nodded. It sounded like a busy life. Perhaps deliberate busy, in order to push out bad memories. While she was still smiling, Barry said, "Can I ask you something?"

Her smile grew. "You want sex after all? We've still got twenty minutes."

Barry could only laugh.

"No, no…I mean…don't get me wrong, that would be nice, but…I just wanted to ask you-"

"What is it, Barry from Ireland?" she asked.

"Why do you do this? Apart from the obvious reasons."

"Apart from the money, you mean. What's a nice girl, and all that?"

Barry smiled awkwardly. "Hope I haven't offended by asking."

"No, Honey", she said, but her smile was fading again. "And you don't mean why do I do it, you mean how can I do it? Ain't that so, Barry?"

He could feel his face redden. How could he not have guessed she'd see right through such a thinly veiled question?

"My folks ain't got much money," she said, "not since the economy went poopy shaped. I soon found out waitressin' don't do much to put a girl through college. Then one day, a friend mentioned this place. Told me she'd been working here for a year or so and the money was great. Then she said she could get me in, that I'd do really well. I looked at her like she'd sprouted another head. Me, a working girl? No way."

"So, what swung you?" asked Barry, fascinated.

"Next semester's fees were comin' up, and this waitress was plumb broke. It took everythin' I had just to eat and pay the rent. So, guess what?"

"You asked your friend for an intro." said Barry.

"Bingo. Nearly pee'd myself when I walked in that door. But Jackie was real nice. Said they only let good clients in. They had to be clean and they had to behave. Nice everyday guys. Guys like you, Barry."

Barry laughed.

"Don't you think I'm a little too well behaved?"

"Ok, so you're not the typical client who walks in here. But, they're just nice fellahs lookin' for a nice time. As long as they pay and don't bring security in here, we don't ask any questions."

She certainly had Barry's interest.

"What if they look like Quasimodo?" he asked.

Kerry got up and pulled a bar of chocolate from a drawer by the bed.

"Ever tried Hersheys?" she asked, offering him a little. He thought he'd asked one question too many. They just sat there, chewing and savoring the confectionery.

"It's good", Barry said, "a little sweeter than I'm used to. But good."

"You mean like the hunchback?"

"What?"

"Quasi-whatshisface."

"Modo", he said,"Quasimodo."

"Yeah, we get plenty of those", she said, looking pensive. "There's this one guy, comes out here once a month or so. Nearly freaked the first time I saw him. He was old, but that didn't bother me. This is no job to be in if you're ageist, believe me. No, this poor guy was livin' in a body that just shouldn't have worked. I mean, he was twisted like spaghetti. Didn't walk, more screwed along like a sidewinder."

"Sounds lovely", said Barry, viewing the mental image forming in his mind.

"Oh, yeah", she said, "and there I was almost helping him along the corridor, cursing him for pickin' me. But what could I do but be nice to him. He'd paid his hundred and fifty, and was expecting his money's worth the same as anyone else. Anyway, we got to my room, and I gotta tell ya, I just didn't know what to offer him. He had a bump on the side of his head like his momma had dropped him when he was a baby. About a hundred times. Some sort of thing, like a mole clung to his chin. Some of his last meal was still stuck there."

Barry wasn't sure if he wanted to hear any more. The Hershey's was making itself felt in his stomach. But there was something compelling in what Kerry was saying.

"So, what happened?"

"Well, if it's one thing I've learned since I started at this, it's that everyone has a redeeming feature, and with this guy, it was his eyes. All blue and soft, they shone out of his face like lights. I remember thinkin' if you could take those eyes and put them on regular guy's face, you could fall in love. And then he started talkin',-'I'm Matt', he said, 'and sweetheart, we don't have to do this if you don't want to."

Barry sat forward, resting his elbows on his knees.

"So, what did you do?"

"Well, he just stood there, and you know what? He looked so sad and pathetic, my heart just melted."

"Pity-sex", said Barry, "the worst kind. Still, it's better than no sex, I suppose."

Kerry frowned. "No, it wasn't like that. There was no pity in it. I can't explain it. Maybe there is no explanation, but something switched in my head. Maybe it was the realization neither of us was in an ideal situation. But not being able to pay the rent was far worse. I realized there and then, George Clooney and Leonardo DiCaprio weren't goin' to be droppin' by with any regularity. It was a case of get on with it, Kerry."

"So, you did", Barry said.

"Yep, and you know, it's not easy gettin' naked with a strange man, much less one you don't fancy. But after a while I could see it goes deeper than providing the facility. For some of them it's harder. They're puttin' themselves on the line. Afraid they might be held up to ridicule. They're makin' a far bigger commitment than I ever will. They stand there, so imperfect. And they've been hurt, you can tell. Some badly. Because they weren't perfect. Didn't fit in. Didn't conform to the world's idea of beauty. No, Honey, I know I felt embarrassed and exposed the first time. But on this stage, you soon realize they're the ones who are far more exposed."

There was profoundness and a sincerity in her words that Barry couldn't add to or question. A little light was exposing some long held notions about prostitution. He was peering across the divide, the fence that kept him on the grounds of so called respectability. It wouldn't be so easy to judge again.

"Do you have a boyfriend?" he ventured, almost immediately regretting the question.

"Sorry", he said, "I'm prying. Don't answer that."

She laughed gently.

"Jeez, Barry, I've told you my life story, why would I hold back on that? I had a boyfriend, a guy from college. He kept tellin' me 'You're the one, Kerry.' And I kept sayin' to myself, 'Wait till you find out about my other life, sweetheart. My alter ego.' He started gettin' real heavy and intense with me, which I didn't really mind. So, I told him everything. Honest Kerry and her conscience."

"What happened?" asked Barry, knowing what the answer was going to be.

"Five minutes later, Mr. Heavy and Intense, Mr. You're The One, was slammin' the door and runnin' like a sheep escapin' the slaughterhouse."

Then she fell into a grey silence.

"I'm sorry", said Barry, trying to dredge up some pearl of wisdom for her. All he found was a pebble of an apology. "I didn't mean to do this to you."

She snapped off another piece of Hershey's and popped it into her mouth. The sound of it breaking up between her teeth filled the room, until she swallowed it hard. Like she was swallowing the truth. Then, finally, she spoke.

"It's ok. The last thing I was expectin' was Barry from Ireland comin' in here tonight and draggin' all this outa me. Seein' as you've come this far, got any advice for a girl like me?"

He looked perplexed, caught out by the question. Barry hated when people asked his advice. They seldom listened, usually doing the opposite of anything he said.

Nonetheless, he offered her whatever his mind conjured in the moment.

"I might", he said, tentatively, "but it won't fix things with your folks. As far as they're concerned, I say fuck them. Sending you away was their loss. Sorry if that shocks you, Kerry, but if they can't accept you as you are, then conditional love isn't love at all. It's shit. Or as we say in Ireland…shite."

His little joke lifted her lips briefly. "Go on…"

"You know what I think you should do? Carry on exactly as you are. If you can make the sad and the lonely feel good about themselves, think how good a physiotherapist you'll be. You have something to give, Kerry, and sex is not the half of it. Can you see what I'm saying?"

She was looking straight at him. Barry couldn't tell if she was going to laugh or cry.

'Jesus, nobody has ever put it like that to me before. Never. Not even my sister. I'm not a bad person, Barry, am I?"

"Never thought that for a second", he said. And he meant it. Kerry had put a human face on something he'd always thought of as sordid. A woman using the most intimate part of her body as a commodity. And some desperate man ready with hard cash and a hard on. A darkened alleyway, putrid with the stench of urine becoming the theatre of a glorious but short lived coupling.

Out on the corridor, voices could be heard. Happy voices, fading as they passed. A man and a woman.

"You come back now, won't ya, sweetie?" she said.

"Oh, you can count on it," he said, "you're an angel, that's what you are."

Kerry smiled at Barry.

"You hear that? We're angels now."

He smiled some more, nodding. "Keep your wings clipped, otherwise the Karma Sutra could get awkward."

He was glad to see she was laughing again.

"You Irish guys always make us laugh."

Then she looked at the clock by the bed. The bed with the sheets still undisturbed.

"I'm sorry, Barry, but the meter's just about run out."

She seemed genuinely saddened by the fact.

"You'll be glad when I'm gone", he said, testing her.

"Uh-uh", she uttered, shaking her head, "I'm glad you came here tonight. I was gettin' doubtful about things. Hell, I even considered goin' back home. Grovellin' on my knees. But you're right. They don't deserve me. As long as I've got my sister, I'll be fine."

Her green eyes were vibrant again, absorbing the smile on her lips.

"Maybe you're some sort of angel yourself, Barry. Sent here to tell me I'll be ok."

He laughed wryly. "Some angel I'd make. But I'm a believer in fate, Kerry. Maybe my reluctant visit was meant to be."

There wasn't much more to be said. The bedside clock seemed to agree, its hands in the midnight position, as if there was a gun pointed at it. Barry got up. He felt the beginnings of a yawn prying at his jaw, but he managed to stifle it.

"Am I your last?" he asked.

Kerry laughed. "Hell, no, Honey, I only started at eight. It's Friday night. I won't get that bed to myself till four or five."

Despite all the talk, he still didn't fully understand how she could do it. Understanding why was easy enough. Survival can take on many guises. And it must have taken a level of detachment that only a woman could muster. But he was certain about one thing. He could not condemn her.

Kerry was on her feet now, stretching and arching her back, before slipping on her shoes.

"C'mon, I'll see you back to the lounge."

She glanced at herself in a mirror, straightening her hair, checking her makeup. Then she applied some lipstick, a deep scarlet, like the buds of her breasts. She saw him in the reflection, watching her.

"You ok, Honey?"

Barry nodded.

Wanna hear somethin' funny?" she asked him.

"What's that?"

"When a guy comes in here, he's supposed to choose one of us. But I chose you. I could see Carla makin' eyes at you. I knew then I had to make my move. Hope you don't mind."

Barry was stunned for a second or two.

"I thought you'd have been glad when I didn't want sex."

Kerry turned from the mirror and faced him. She looked serious, though not sad like before. It was more a look of intent, radiating from her eyes and seeping into every part of her pretty face.

"You know", she said, "I really would have liked doin' it with you."

Her words hit Barry like a spray of gunfire. A new kind of nervousness rose within him. A feeling that made him wish he was single again. Just for a while. A glorious moment where wife and children didn't exist. It was nice to feel wanted by a woman other than Kate, especially one like this girl. Sometimes he regretted that he'd not played the field a bit before meeting Kate. The file marked 'Previous Conquests' languished noticeably empty in his mind. And it wasn't that he'd never had any offers. But once Kate had caught his sixteen year old eyes, his fate was sealed, his heart marked "sold'. And it still bore the tag twenty-odd years later. But, there were still those moments. He couldn't deny it, but this might have been one of them. The clock issued a discreet bleep. Just enough to say the meter had finally run out. Kerry shrugged her shoulders.

"That's us, I guess, Barry."

"Will you be ok?" he asked.

It felt strange to be asking. What the hell was he going to do if she said no. Go and meet her father? Plead her case? But he did feel concerned for her. He couldn't help it. He wondered was it the father in him. If Kate had fell pregnant after they'd met, their own daughter would be about Kerry's age now.

"I'm fine", she said, "really."

And there it was again. The smile that engaged every part of her face. If it was put on, then she was a worthy actor. He made for the door, placing his hand on the handle. Turning round, he found she was standing close to him. So close, her scent danced in the tunnels of his nose. Sweet perfume. Heady. Tempting, like the first sweets after lent. The green of her eyes fascinated him. Was this how men felt when they looked at Medusa?

"Hey", she said, "think your wife would mind if I kissed you?"

Barry's heart lurched, like it had scurried into his stomach.

"You said you weren't allowed to kiss the clients", he said.

"We're not. But you're not a client, Barry. Not in my eyes, at least."

Her voice was an octave or so lower and it played on his ears like rolling waves.

"You won't catch anything", she assured him, "it's a rule I never break…until now."

"Yes, but I'm marr-."

Her lips suddenly landed on his, swallowing his words. He could taste the lipstick, flavoured like fruit, waxen on the brim of her mouth. The voice in his head telling him to push her away was soon silenced by another urging him to close his eyes. Surrender to the hypnosis. The flesh of her lips, the skin of her face brushing against his. It was strange, beautiful, exciting, wrong, so very wrong, yet exquisite. Her taste, her scent, seeped through him like anaesthesia. He thought of Adam and suddenly knew how the poor bastard must have felt. Here was Eve, real and alive, the apple fresh from the tree. An apple Barry knew he had to resist. But not just yet. He and Kerry breathed through their noses, affording the kiss all the time it needed.

Desperately, he wanted to caress the curves of her body, to satisfy that part of a man's mind that wanders into unchartered waters. That wonders what it's like to sow seed in a field that doesn't belong to him. He cupped his hands about her face, allowing the silken flax of her golden hair to fall through his fingers. He eventually opened his eyes. Kerry's were still closed, like she'd lost track of everything. A sudden knock on the door shocked them both back to reality.

"You ok in there, Kerry?"

It was Jackie. Barry glanced at the clock. Ten past midnight.

"Oh, sure, Jackie, be right there."

The woman's footsteps trailed away. Kerry's arms were still resting on Barry's shoulders. His heart was finding a regular pace again.

"That was nice", she said, "real nice."

He nodded, half smiling. Guilt was knocking on the door of his mind. But it wasn't exactly kicking it in either. Fuck it, he thought. He could talk it over with guilt later. Send it on its way.

"I'd better go", he told her, "I'm getting you into trouble."

She led him back along the corridor, back to the lounge area. She held his hand the whole way.

The other girls were already there, chatting to new arrivals from the world outside. Tom and Rob were already waiting there, looking at Barry in disbelief. Had he really gone through with it?

While they were still a little way off, Kerry whispered to him.

"Thanks, Irish Barry. I feel a whole lot better 'bout things."

"Good", he said. "You've nothing to feel bad about. Keep up the studies and don't lose touch with your sister."

"Ok."

"I had a nice time, Kerry, I mean it."

She gave him a peck on the cheek and joined the other girls.

"Are you right, Romeo?" said Tom.

As they left, Kerry threw Barry a little wave. He waved back, her face imprinting on his mind as they turned the corner and made for the exit.

"Jesus, would you look at this", said Feeney, "yer man's in love."

Barry glowered at him. "I came to your fuckin' club, didn't I? Now shut the fuck up."

Tom wobbled his head sarcastically. "Aw, yeah, thanks Tom for a great time. Sure it only cost you three hundred bucks."

Barry ignored him.

"Goodnight, guys", the doorman said, and then they were back on the street again. The drizzle had turned to full blown rain, drumming on the pavement. Tom pulled his collar round his neck.

"There's a taxi", he said.

It pulled up outside the club. Its interior was full of men with dollars and desires. The lads waited as one of the occupants settled the fare with the driver.

"Jesus, that was sweet", said Tom, I'm definitely comin' back the next time we're here."

"All I want to do is get into this taxi", said Rob, wiping rainwater from his face.

Finally, the doors opened, and the eager passengers began to emerge. As the last man got, he paused and spoke.

"Tom, is that you?"

For the first time all night, Feeney was struck by silence. After a moment, some awkward words formed in his throat.

"Heh…Frank…what are you doin' here?"

The man's eyebrows locked into a frown. He pointed at one of his party.

"It's his first time in the States. We're here on business. Thought we'd show him this place."

He looked at his companions. "Go on in, I'll be there in a minute."

They left. Then Barry and Rob slid onto the back seat of the taxi, leaving Tom and Frank facing each other in the rain like cowboys about to draw guns. Tom sounded like he was the one whose gun was jammed.

"I…I was…we were-"

"You know what kind of place this is, don't you?" Frank demanded.

Through the open door, Barry and Rob listened intently from the shadowy interior. Tom looked totally incredulous that this Frank fellow, whoever he was, had suddenly shown up like this. Finally, his words stopped dissolving like candy floss in his mouth.

"Ah, just brought these lads down for a mooch around. Entertainin' the troops. You know, a bit like yourself there."

Tom was saying words Frank wasn't buying. The guy glanced into the cab at Barry and Rob, his eyes probing like a Grand Inquisitor. Then he faced Feeney again.

See ya", he told him, darkly, before striding through the rain toward the club.

Tom got into the car, slamming the door shut.

"Fuck, fuck, fuck."

He thumped the dashboard. "Fuck."

"Hey, watch it, Buddy", the driver said, before moving off.

"Who was that, Tom?" asked a bewildered Rob.

Tom squeezed clumps of his hair with his hands.

"I don't believe it. The fuckin' size of America and I had to run into him here."

"Will you just tell us who the hell he is", said Barry, "You're making it sound like he's your worst enemy."

Tom swung round and faced them. "He could turn out to be. He's my brother-in-law. Can you believe that? Mary's fuckin' brother. Aw, Jesus."

He started grabbing at his hair again. "Me and me fuckin' dick. I knew it would get me into trouble some day, but not like this."

"Calm down", said Rob, "He's hardly likely to say anything. Sure, wasn't he goin' into that place himself."

Tom looked at him menacingly.

"He's not married. No girlfriend worth talking about. Don't you see? He can do whatever the hell he wants."

"Oh", said Rob, with sudden understanding.

The driver, the same one who'd brought them out there, was smiling to himself. Barry could imagine him telling the other drivers about the stupid Irishman who'd been caught with his trousers down three thousand miles from home, and those drivers breaking into a chorus of 'Ole- ole-ole! Ole- ole.'

"What are you going to do?" he asked Tom.

"We're gettin' on the first flight outa here in the morning, that's what."

"What about Shortalls?" said Rob. "Ten in the morning, that's what you said, Tom."

"To hell with Shortalls", was the response, "I want to get back to Ireland before that fucker does, spilling beans like an earthquake at a Heinz factory."

He was getting more and more agitated. The other two thought it best to say no more.

The image of the black ledger in the club's reception came back into Barry's head. It seemed the Devil had gotten his hands on the thing already. As Tom sat up front chewing his nails, little memories were coming back to Barry. Memories Barry knew would never leave him. Kerry's face was everywhere. In the rain sodden streets, in the shop windows, under bright lights and in shadowy corners. There'd been talk of angels, and Barry reckoned that's what she had to be, casting light through a smokey sky. Reaching out to lost and lonely souls. Like the old man. Disabled, physically and emotionally. Reject- ed. Craving love and tenderness. To feel not so much like a normal man, but any kind of man. Just for an hour. And Kerry was there, her angel wings folded about the wretched soul, like a force field, keeping out the squalid world.

Tom was slumped back in the seat, rubbing his head like someone nursing migraine. Barry imagined him thinking up excuses, his mind working like a frantic press, printing money, most of it counterfeit. Just like the man himself. Feeney annoyed Barry. Endlessly. But he didn't hate him enough to hope his wife would kick him out, or rather, get her brother to do it for her. Men like Tom Feeney made life hard on themselves. Never content, a façade of arrogance and playing the big fellow hiding a myriad of insecurities.

The streets started to look familiar again. Soon the hotel would come into view. Rob had nodded off, his head resting against the window, mouth open. If Tom hadn't been so preoccupied with his impending execution, he would have ribbed him mercilessly, telling him he had no stamina and asking had the girl worn him out.

It had been a weird and eventful night, and it was only now Kate came to Barry's mind. He hadn't phoned her. A quick totting up of time zones told him it was only 9pm in Ireland. Not too late.

The taxi pulled up at the hotel. Tom jumped out with the words, "we're getting' out of this kip first thing", leaving Barry to settle the fare and prod the slumbering Rob back to life.

In his room, Barry slumped on a chair, sipping strong tea. The call to Kate had been a little stilted.

"Are you ok?" she'd wanted to know.

"Tired, love, just tired. It's one a.m. here. Had a long …meeting, that's all."

He could have told her. Told her about Feeney railroading him into going to this club. And how he'd gone along with it, pathetically. And there was this girl. Remind you of our Sarah, she would. Just a little older. Told me all about her life. He could have said it, and she'd have believed him, because they trusted each other. But the kiss. That lingering, sweet kiss.

What'll you do about that, Barry? he wondered. What could he do, but file it in the vault marked 'secrets'. God knew, it was empty enough in there. A lifetime of being good old dependable, honest Barry. It grated, sometimes. Had he ever lived at all? Never straying from what was expected of him. Family man. Feed, clothe, educate. Provide a roof. Service the car, clear the gutters on a Saturday. Two weeks in Portugal every year. Wasn't it time that echo-y vault had something in it to accompany him into old age? That for one moment, long ago, he dared to forget who he was, just for the briefest of moments.

But it was Kate he wanted now. Kate he missed. Despite the years, it was she who still excited him. He was glad they were leaving in the morning. That Shortalls was off. This time tomorrow, he'd be home. She'd be glad to see him. Kate always was. Better get some nice perfume at the duty free. Maybe some Chanel. And tomorrow night, after they'd chatted into the small hours, they'd fall into bed exhausted, their minds meandering into sleep. He'd cup her breast with his hand. Nothing sexual, just comfort. A breast that may have lost some of its youthful pertness, but had nurtured his three children. They'd lay like that for ages, her and him, fitting together. Warm in the womb of the bed. And in the morning, late, she'd blow in his ear, gently, till he woke.

"Where's my Sunday sausage?" she'd ask.

It was their little joke. Had been for years. He'd smile at her, playing with her hair, strewn haphazardly about the pillow. Through all of this, Barry never once thought of Kerry. Never once made any comparisons, and he was glad.

From the balcony, he watched the cars like dots on the streets be-low. It was true. New York was a city with insomnia.

As he got ready for bed, Barry thought of the black ledger at the club. He imagined the Devil thumbing through it, and coming to his name. And the night he signed it would be called into question. What would Satan say? What could he say to a man who'd been tempted by an angel?

End

THE LONELINESS OF
A BUSY STREET

The Loneliness Of A Busy Street

*J*ack Collins lifted the lace curtain and peered out at the terraced houses. A marmalade moon hung low on the horizon, its edges softened by a misty sky. The street was quiet, eerily so. The flicker of T.V.s filtered through curtains in darkened sitting rooms. Neighbours vegetating in front of soaps, caricatures of their own lives. How they didn't confuse one with the other, he never knew. What he did know, was that Hawthorn Avenue's ghostly silence would be shattered to-morrow night. Jack hated Halloween. It was usually nothing but trouble for the locals, the annual dread.

He lowered the net and turned on the lamp by the armchair. A Boxer dog looked up at him, loyalty already formed in her young eyes. Jack patted her head.

"Well, Millie, you, me, and the world are a year older." He laughed softly. "You and the world can afford to squander another year. I can't."

The dog wagged its rump as if it had a tail.

Jack smiled.

"Haven't a clue, have ye, Millie? Might as well be recitin' the Rosary."

In the morning, October sunlight drenched the ancient, arthritic brickwork of Hawthorn Terrace. Sixty years, a marriage and three pregnancies had all played out at number twelve. So long ago. Youth and vitality in plentiful supply, stretching toward a horizon Jack never bothered looking at.

The dog sat by the front door, watching Jack shoulder himself into a heavy coat. "Not today, Millie", he told her, "they'll not let you into the shops."

As if understanding, the dog traipsed to her basket, curling up like a hairy spring.

The sun had been deceptive. A chill tore at Jack's asthma ravaged lungs. When he reached the main street, he warmed himself with tea in Chandler's Café. From its window, he looked onto at a street that had changed little over the years, shops refusing to submit to the granite and glass sweeping out from the rejuvenating city centre. Only their business changed. What had been Doyle's Bakery was now a mobile phone outlet, where track-suited youths and trendy mothers were tended by slim girls and boys coaxing beards from spotty faces. Johnsons, who'd proudly proclaimed themselves as gentleman's outfitters for a century, was now gone, replaced by a computer shop.

Jack preferred not to think about it. The world was condensing, submitting to the silicon chip, and it was leaving him behind. As long as O'Casey Street held on to a shred of familiarity on the outside, he didn't care.

1954. November.

It was an odd month for a wedding, but Maura's mother didn't look like she'd live till the spring. Maura worried about bringing the wedding forward.

"They'll think I'm pregnant", she told Jack, coming home from the pictures one night.

At the reception, she glanced at her mother constantly, a salmon coloured outfit doing little to disguise its contents of a pale and fragile woman.

The hotel fronted toward the sea, ruffled by winter winds. Fr. Mc-Gettigan stayed sober long enough to say a few words at the top table. At dusk, Jack's brothers carried him off the beach, like troops shouldering the wounded at Normandy.

The newlyweds flew into London that night. The city was soaked in fog, the blanket of gloop stabbed by shards of orange lamplight. The captain announced they were lucky. The plasma of fog was growing and no more planes would land until tomorrow.

"15 Eddington Road", Jack told a taxi driver.

Maura's aunt and uncle couldn't make the wedding, but had offered to put them up for the week. The old boy had phoned, talking about the spare room, and what was the point of wasting money on a hotel. To Jack's annoyance, Maura jumped at it, saying she hadn't seen the Hopkins in years.

Norman Hopkins, stout and balding, ushered them into the warm parlour, where his wife waited with tea and hugs. All Jack could think of was getting his new wife to bed. To initiate married life. He'd coaxed her during their courting, but Maura was having none of it.

Fr. McGettigan had had a talk with her, in the presence of her mother and father. Between sips of her father's whiskey, he said, "Save yourself for your husband, dear. God can wait for anything, and so must you. Far too many Godless girls in the mother and baby homes. You don't want to end up like now, do you?"

It was enough to frighten Maura into surrendering nothing more than kisses to Jack, always diverting his eager, wandering hands. But now, tonight, in the Hopkins' spare room, the famine would be over.

Old Norman wittered on about carpentry and pigeons, and why the Ford Prefect was better than the Morris Oxford. Jack curled his toes and stifled yawns and watched twenty-one year old Maura smile and run fingers through her hair as she chatted to Ellen on the settee.

At midnight, an outbreak of yawning prompted the Hopkins to go to bed. The aunt showed the newlyweds to their room. Small, tidy, faint smell of mould. She gave her niece another hug, said extra blankets were in the wardrobe, and then she was gone.

The room fell silent, a distant whistle of a train cutting the musky air. Jack could hear the memories of the day play out in his head, and he smiled at Maura. Their moment had come, and he didn't know what to say to her. Wedding braids still adorned her hair. He thought she'd never looked lovelier.

When she returned from the bathroom, he was in bed, patting the empty side. He wanted to say something to her. Anything. To know she was as anxious as he was. And as willing.

His hands were like calves exploring new pastures, tramping through the meadow of her body. He felt her tense. Through whispers, she urged him slow down. But the desires of Jack's barren courtship could no longer be abated, becoming moans he tried to subdue. The old bed joined in, creaking springs goading him on. His release came amid images of the Hopkins listening behind the wall, and Maura's sickly mother looking in the window. Fr. McGettigan raised a Glenfiddich.

Jack looked down at Maura. Twenty-one year old Maura. Now a conquered woman, her eyes awash with indifference. He took up his side of the bed again. Maura laid her head on his chest, on his racing heart. His mind sifted and stumbled through countless words, none of them worth using.

A toilet flushed. Old Norman huffed back to the bedroom. Through the wall, muffled voices. Then silence. Jack could feel Maura thaw and soften in his arms.

"We should gone have to a hotel", he whispered.

In the half light, she smiled, shaking her head.

"It's fine."

He wondered how it had been for her. Wanted to ask her, but didn't know how. Had he hurt her? Been too rough? Too fast? Christ, Maura, say something.

Grey London fog heaved against the window. A cat screamed. Their moment was over.

On the main street, Jack struggled against a world that going the other way. He stepped aside for a girl, pacing like tomorrow wasn't going to come, mobile phone pressed to her ear. She looked through him like he didn't exist.

"I'm tellin' ye, Mary, they're not takin' me social welfare. I'll pull yer wan through the bleedin' hatch when I go down there."

He took up the trek again. A familiar face emerged from the throng.

"Jack Collins, is that you? Haven't seen you in ages."

The woman stopped, and the crowds slipped past her and Jack like minnows.

"Breda", he said, "how the devil are you? How's that grandson of yours? Is he a doctor yet?"

Breda Mallin smiled and nodded.

"One more year, then he's off to Africa."

"Good for him. Maura was always very fond of him. So, how've you been keeping yourself?"

He studied her face. "You're a great colour, Breda. Were you away?"

Her expression changed.

"Ah, I'm cut with cancer."

Her words speared Jack.

"What? Jesus, Breda, I didn't know."

She shrugged.

"The liver, they tell me. And me that never drank. The Pioneer pin didn't do me much good, eh?"

She laughed dryly at her own remarks, and Jack didn't know what to say. What had looked like the remnants of a holiday tan a moment ago was now the amber warning of early-stage liver failure. His stupidity was gift-wrapped in embarrassment. Breda lived at the end the terrace, but it might well have been a hundred miles away. One of the last things Maura had told him before Dementia tore her mind asunder, torpedoed into his head.

"Don't lose touch with the old neighbours. The Mallins are here as long as us, and Breda's a good sort. I know you, Jack Collins. You'd sit in all day, watchin' the racing channel." He'd promised he'd do no such thing, and here he was, bumping into Breda Mallin by accident a year later, curling his toes with embarrassment. She and Ted had called more than once after Maura died, but Jack had pretended he wasn't in, peeping through the lace like a fugitive.

"I have to go", she finally said.

Jack willed his brain to supply something wise and consoling, but the stupid old thing just sat in his head like a flat battery.

"I'll come over, Breda. Say hello to Ted."

She nodded, and he watched as the crowd took her. He could hear

Maura in his mind, scolding.

"I told you, didn't I? All the years she was our friend, and you had to find out like that. Stupid old fool."

Stupid. Stupid. Stupid.

The supermarket was busy. Friday shoppers with wages in their bank accounts thronged the aisles. Jack took out a meagre list. Shopping for one, a lonely occupation.

Bread.

He picked up two loaves.

Soda bread or garlic bread?

He could hear Maura again.

"Soda. You know I can't stand garlic."

Smiling, he put down the soda bread, and threw the garlic loaf into his little trolley.

Milk.

Two women chatted by the fridge. There'd been a school reunion, apparently.

"Pamela Johnson turned up. Still a bitch, looking down on everyone."

The other one was agog, Dairygold in hand.

"What did she say?"

"Asked if my husband was still a coalman. And did we still live in a council estate. Then pretended to get my name wrong. It's been so long, she said."

"What did you say to that?"

"Never mind, Pamela, what you lost in looks, you gained in weight."

The other one laughed, and Jack wanted to as well. 'Good for you', he wanted to say, but they'd only look at him crooked. A leering old man with a tartan trolley and its miserable rations.

At the till, he emptied the contents onto the conveyer. The girl was chatty enough, but, amidst commenting on the weather, she slyly leaned forward, checking the little cart for undeclared goods. Jack was old, a pin-up boy for curved spine and arthritis, but he wasn't stupid. Tilting the trolley forward, he said, "It's empty. Do you think I'm a thief?"

Her face reddened.

"You should use the trolleys or baskets provided, sir."

He glared at her with steely eyes. Eyes still sharp. Eyes that had seen more than her's ever had. In one severe look, her words were diminished. The bleep of the scanner knifed the silence. Until she demanded twenty-one euro and nine cent.

1963. Winter.

"Someone close his mouth."

Maura stood looking at her freshly-dead father, jaws prised open, like the man finally had something to say, and it was too late.

Jack called the nurse, who did her best to close the recalcitrant mandible.

"Rigor Mortis, already", she declared, "I'll get the orderly to do something."

Maura and her sister left the room, leaving their brothers forming a silent, awkward guard round the bed. From the doorway of the small room, Jack watched Maura and Kathleen at the end of the corridor. He wanted to go to Maura, to put his arms around her and console her. But something stopped him. The women stood silently, not a single, cold tear between them. They exchanged occasional glances, but stared mainly at the grey, polished floor. The oddness of it struck Jack, but he dismissed it. When their mother died eight years previously, Jack watched the sisters cry for three solid days. Wasn't their old father worth at least a few tears? Maura's face was like a blank mask. Jack recognized that look. One night, years ago, during sex, he opened his eyes to see her face, silvered by a spoke of moonlight, her eyes wide and staring. It had unnerved him, and it disturbed him now.

He felt bad not going to her, but some sort of wall surrounded the women, within which there seemed to be an unspoken kindredship. It seemed to go beyond the unity of grieving sisters. Whatever it was, it didn't require tears.

A spear of orange sunlight crept into the corridor. The night vigil was over, and with it, seventy-four years of a man's life.

Jack couldn't wait any longer. Maura and Kathleen put on new faces as he approached.

"I'm sorry", he told them.

Half-smiles twisted their mouths, and they nodded.

The nurse reappeared, telling them their father was much better. Jack smiled at her choice of words.

"The orderly's finished now", she said, "you can go back in."

When she went away, Maura said, "Jack, take me home."

"Are you not going back in?" he wanted to know.

Her face stiffened.

"The lads can stay. I'll see him when they bring him home."

Jack looked at Kathleen, who responded with a smile that refused to infect her eyes.

Maura's footsteps echoed in the corridor.

Jack normally had lunch in Bannon's Bar on a Friday, but the checkout girl had soured him. He tugged the little trolley through the growing hordes, deciding it was best to get home. The dog would be anxious and hungry.

At the corner of Court Street, he waited for the green man to appear. When it did, he set off. He was still halfway across the junction when a white van rounded the corner, clipping the trolley and tearing it from his grip. Jack spun round, lost his footing and fell to the ground. The last thing he saw before blacking out was the van disappear into the distance.

1972. Bloody Sunday.

The TV rattled as another explosion shook its frame. Maura held Kevin, one week old, drawing the blanket round him as if the set was about to spew its scenes into the living-room. Niamh and Anthony looked worried.

"Is that Dublin, Mummy?" Niamh asked.

"No, pet, it's far away. Nothing for you to worry about."

Maura signaled with frowning eyes at Jack to turn off the TV. When he did, a sudden silence fell over the room.

"You don't think that stuff could start down here?" she whispered to Jack.

"I hope not", he said, "it's getting' worse and no mistake."

He took the baby from her arms, and held him aloft.

"A little miracle, that's what you are."

The infant gurgled, looking into his father's eyes as if he understood. Indeed, the baby was a miracle of sorts, born out a coupling that was becoming ever scarcer. The marital bed was now mainly a place of rest. Over time, Maura had become adept at choosing from a menu of reasons why sex should be put off for another night. A headache, a backache, two children to run after and now a baby. It was hard for Jack to argue his case. Not without sounding like a sex-crazed rapist. That he loved her and desired her in equal measure that was all. Couldn't she see that? He was a man, a simple Irish man. Catholic. Not programmed for such conversations. Ask his wife why she didn't much like sex, and performed it like one of the household chores?

Not bloody likely.

Instead, he took refuge in Bannon's bar. In Guinness and darts. And men dispensing drink-fuelled wisdom. Something was festering in his marriage, refusing to crust over and heal.

On the Monday, the phone rang. It was Maura's eldest brother, Tom. It was their father's birthday remembrance, and should he put a notice in the paper?

Jack overheard Maura's side of the conversation. Long gaps as Tom spoke, punctuated by vague lip service from her.

"Whatever you think, Tom." "Yeah, that's grand." "No, don't bother asking Kathleen." "Word it whatever way you want."

And there it was again. The old unsolved equation. The one that wouldn't add up. Not least because Jack simply wouldn't allow it to. The answer was an elephant, trying to squeeze into a room that could never hold it.

More than once, coming home from Bannon's, his courage buoyed by drink, Jack had resolved to prod Maura from her sleep and ask her what it was all about. How could anyone be so cold to their father? Sure, he wasn't an affectionate man, but that wasn't reason enough to cold shoulder him. And what about Kathleen? Why was she the same? What was this conspiracy? What had old Christy Millar done? Millar, the bible basher. Millar, the greengrocer, stocking images of the Sacred Heart among the carrots and cauliflours. The only greengrocer in Dublin who wouldn't sell apples because they'd tempted Adam and Eve.

Jack would arrive home, and the Dutch courage would be gone, pissed away in some alley. Maura would be asleep, at least she'd look like she was. Asking bold questions now would be like shooting into a darkened wood, scattering crows in all directions, caw-cawing, ruffling their wings on gnarled branches. And the damned creatures might never settle again. No, Jack, best leave it. And he did, incarcerating his suspicions about his father-in-law in a tomb at the back of his mind.

The wailing of an ambulance brought Jack round. That and the anxious, murmuring crowd that surrounded him.

"He's coming to", someone said, "he must have banged his head when he fell, poor divel."

A woman held his hand.

"Are you alright, love? Don't try to move."

Her hand felt warm. Soft. A child stood by her side.

"Is he alright. Mammy?"

"He's shivering", a man said, taking his coat off and draping it over Jack.

The siren got louder, then stopped as the ambulance arrived. A woman in a green uniform crouched beside Jack, while her colleague asked the crowd to step away.

"I'm Judy", she said, shining a light in his eyes, "what happened?"

"Some upstart in a van", Jack relayed, "flew round that corner and…the shopping. Where's the trolley?"

"It's alright, mister", a youth said, I have it here. It's a bit twisted, though."

"Never mind that", the paramedic said, "it's you we have to worry about."

She took his blood pressure, while the other one prodded his legs.

"Can you move your feet?" he asked.

Jack complied, though it took a little effort. His breathing was becoming labored.

"Let's get him into the ambulance", Judy said, satisfied Jack had no serious injuries.

They maneuvered him onto a stretcher. A mask was placed on his face, and soothing oxygen filled his lungs.

"Asthma? Judy asked.

He nodded.

She was in her late thirties, or so Jack guessed. Slim figured, chest-nut hair tucked behind one ear. He thought she was pretty, a slip of a girl to an eighty-four year old.

The oxygen mined the depths of his chest, relaxing him, lightening his mind.

"Twenty years ago," he thought, watching her as she stretched, putting the equipment away.

Then he laughed to himself. "Maybe thirty."

Of course, Jack knew he would have done no such thing. Not to Maura. In youth and old age, he'd loved her dearly. Through the sex-ual drought that had robbed them both of so much. That parched his desires. His needs. They could have known another side of each other. But Maura never seemed to have those needs. In the rare times when she'd tried to let go, to give herself to him, there was a hint of what could have been. But he always sensed the resistance, springing from deep within her, with the tension of a rat trap. And in his head, the reasoning that he couldn't put into words. The reasoning of a man who didn't really understand.

"C'mon Maura, you might enjoy it. Christ, it's only a bit of sex. It's meant to be fun."

"Are you ok, Jack?" Judy asked.

He nodded, the gas massaging the pipes of his old lungs.

She was just about to close the ambulance door and signal her partner to set off, when another uniform appeared. A young Garda, haircut like velcro, peered over at Jack.

"How is he? Could I ask him a few questions?"

"Just for a few seconds" Judy said, "we want to get him away."

The cop mounted the step and leaned over Jack, radio crackling on his shoulder. He made Jack recount the incident, taking notes as he spoke.

"Did you get the registration of the van?"

The ancient furrow between Jack's eyes deepened.

"Get his number? I was lucky to get off the bloody road alive. The van was white, that's all I know."

The cop pressed on.

"Any markings? Sign writing?"

Jack coughed, making Judy bring the interrogation to an end.

"He needs to be checked out properly. You have his address."

As the Garda left, the youth handed over Jack's trolley, having saved what he could. The paramedic thanked him, then closed the door. As the ambulance moved off, she drew the blanket over Jack's shoulders and smiled. He felt more comfortable now, which irritated him slightly. All he craved nowadays was comfort and warmth. The manliness of his body was gone, laboured away on winter-ravaged building sites.

The casualty department was like the aftermath of a small battle. Behind a curtain, a woman moaned.

"Can you hear me, Mary?" a nurse said. "Mary... Mary?"

The doctor sounded concerned.

"She needs to be pumped out, and fast."

Jack wanted to get out of there. The dog would be frantic. An image of a chewed up armchair urged him to call the nurse.

"Are you alright, Jack?" she said.

"I am. I need to get home."

The nurse looked flustered. "You have to be checked over first. As soon as we're done with this lady, the doctor will be with you."

For twenty minutes, Jack listened to a foreign doctor, an Irish nurse and an overdosed Dubliner having the contents of her stomach ejected.

In little bays all around him, doctors and nurses tended the troops of life. War weary, the weekend wounded, with their torn ligaments, snapped bones and chest pains. And above it all, somebody called Mary, heaving, returning pills and whiskey to daylight.

Jack tried to sympathize, but if it hadn't been for her, he might have been released by now. Eventually, Mary's suffering gave way to some coherence. It sounded like she knew the nurse.

"Could you not have let me be, Aileen? I'll finish the job next time. I'll do it proper, I'm tellin' ye."

The nurse urged her to rest. Jack could hear her and the doctor leave the cubicle. They spoke in lowered tones, as if their voices couldn't penetrate the flimsy screen.

"You know this woman?" the doctor asked.

"Yes, we grew up together. She's in here every couple of months."

There was a rustle of paper.

"Yes, I see there's a history of this. Any idea why?"

She hesitated a moment, lowering her voice further. Jack strained his ears.

"Abuse. Her father ended up in prison."

"Sexual?" the doctor asked, saying it like it was just another disease.

The nurse said nothing, but Jack imagined her nodding.

Then he froze.

There it was again. The equation. Adding up with horrid precision. The answer confirmed correct by this woman called Mary. Years of naivety and denial washed away in casualty on a Friday afternoon.

Suddenly, the madness of the place was unnoticeable. Jack had never heard so much silence. And in the midst of it, Maura's voice. On their wedding night. "Easy, Jack. Slow down."

And on the tearless dawn of her father's death. "Take me home, Jack."

Now, in the battlefield of this hospital, Jack was finally waking up, horrible realizations creeping over his withered body, and settling in his tired mind. He thought of his own daughter, the one girl he and Maura had given the world. And he wondered how he could have done anything else but loved her. Held and hugged her child's body in his arms, shielding her from the evils of the world. Gentle goodnight kisses on the forehead after bedtime stories. He willed his mind to imagine forcing some torrid act upon her innocence, but his kindly old soul wouldn't allow him to glimpse the world through Christy Millar's eyes. For that Jack was glad.

The nurse finally returned. "Jack, you shouldn't have taken that off."

The mask was now in his hand, hissing oxygen like a wounded bagpipes. "I feel ok", he said, "can I go home?"

Before she could answer, the doctor strode in, notes in hand, and Jack had to explain the whole thing again. The African umm-ed and ah-ed, then listened to Jack's old lungs with a stethoscope. "Did you knock your head?"

"No, I don't think so…maybe…I wasn't out for long."

A light reflected off the steel-grey of Jack's eyes.

"You don't appear to be concussed."

"I'll go home, so"

The doctor ignored him.

"Raise your arms, please", and he checked Jack's limbs for mobility. Did the vehicle make contact with you?"

"No. Made shit of the groceries, though. All over the bloody road."

The doctor nodded again, smiled, then declared Jack could be discharged.

In the taxi home, Jack remembered the woman in the next cubicle. Her history had finally made him face up to his own, or rather, Maura's. He'd caught a glimpse of her as he left, poor creature. Dark haired and thirty-something, she reminded him of Maura at that age. Except Maura had bore her sufferings differently. By day, a loving mother, a smiling wife. It was the menace of night that brought on her demons. He could see that now. That hushed chat between doctor and nurse had brought back dormant suspicions about old Millar. Suspicions that were now confirmations. Two plus two finally made four. Fifty years too late. Hatred drizzled over

Jack, soaking his thoughts with the want for revenge. The best he could hope for now was that the bastard was burning in the hell he'd so often spoken of.

The taxi drew up outside number twelve. At the end of Hawthorn

Terrace, a pillar of pallets and planks, topped with a crown of tyres, was silhouetted against the dying sun. He'd forgotten it was Halloween, and the dread of it set in again. Soon, the war would begin. The whistle and bang of a distant firework was like a warning. Once inside, Jack bolted the door. The dog jumped and ran circles round him, panting and yelping.

"Millie, Millie, did you think I wasn't coming home?"

Thankfully, the furniture was intact. A pool of urine by the back door was all that had to be contended with. Jack lit the fire, whilst Millie savaged a bowl of nuts, pricking her ears every so often as more fireworks cut into the night. The Halloween hooligans were on the rise.

There was a knock on the door. The dog lifted her head and growled. Jack peered through a crack in the curtains. The outside light illuminated Casper the Ghost and a headless something or other. Both had carrier bags full of monkey nuts and sweets. The mother of the two abominations stood behind them.

"Ah, would you look at that, Millie. I'd better get them something."

He retrieved crisps from the kitchen and unlocked the front door.

"Trick or treat, trick or treat."

The monsters feigned menace, but Jack could only smile at their innocence.

"Hello, Sandra", he said, adding the crisps to the treasury.

"Hello, Jack. Just doing the rounds before the big ones take over the street for the night."

He envied the woman. She had a burly husband to deal with alcohol soaked youths.

A sudden bang made everyone jump as a firework bounced over the lawn, sparks flickering in its wake. The mother began laughing, eliciting giggles from the children. But Jack's heart dipped into his stomach. The memory of one of those things posted through the letter flap and exploding in the hall two years ago came back. Maura, marooned in another world by dementia, screamed with terror. It took an hour to calm her down, Jack eventually phoning Breda Mallin for help. The children came home from abroad after that. Maura was dead within the month.

A volley of fireworks coloured the sky. Jack watched a moment with Sandra and the children, then bid them goodnight, deciding he wasn't going to open the door again.

"Ah, Millie, will this night ever end...Millie? Where are you?"

The box in the corner was empty.

Panic gripped Jack as he scanned the dimly lit reaches of the room. No Millie. The kitchen was also a blank.

"Millie", he called, over and over, the realization that she was gone, creeping over him.

"Aw, Christ, she must have scarpered when I was gawpin' at them bloody fireworks."

He looked out the window. There wasn't a sign of the young boxer, and the first of the teenagers were claiming the street. One lad slung a sports bag over his shoulder, pregnant with rockets and bangers. His mate downed the dregs of a beer can, then tossed it onto the ground. Its aluminum skin rattled on the road. The sound of anarchy.

Jack cursed the dog for escaping, and fretted for her safety at the same time. He'd have to go and look for her. He'd heard too much about what drunken youths did to pets on fireworks night.

He threw on his coat, looking out at the street as he did so. The green glowed as flames took hold of the bonfire. A dozen or so teens, boys and girls, stood round it like druids and witches, jeering. He took a puff of his inhaler to shore up his lungs against the smoky air outside, unbolted the door and presented himself to the battlefield.

A plethora of fireworks tore into the blackness, sprinkling the sky red and green. For a moment, Jack was hypnotized by the luminescence.

"Millie…Millie."

He imagined her yelping, cowering under a hedge, perhaps. Too scared to come out. But she was nowhere near. As he swung open the garden gate, he found his exit blocked by two lads. One stood behind the other, half hidden by shadows. He held something, but Jack couldn't make out what. They wore hoodies, and to Jack they looked like evil monks.

"Hey, Mister."

Jack retreated a couple of steps.

"What? What do you want?"

The youths advanced, crossing the threshold of the garden.

"Is this yours, Mister?"

The speaker came out of the shadows, allowing the streetlamp to show what he carried.

"Millie", said Jack, "oh my God, where did you find her?"

The lad handed the half-grown boxer over. She barked and licked Jack's face, like she hadn't seen him for a month.

"The other side of the green. It said number twelve on the collar, so…"

"So you brought her back. Thanks, lads. Thank you so much."

"Ah, that's alright, Mister. The other lads helped us round her up. We'd hate to see anything happen to her, you know, with the fireworks and all."

The other fellow remained quiet, clutching a battery of beer cans. The hoods shrouding their faces didn't seem so intimidating now. Nor could they hide the sincerity of their eyes.

"Wait a minute, lads."

Jack went inside, put Millie in the sitting room, and reappeared with two packets of crisps.

"To go with the beer", he said, smiling.

"Ah, thanks, Mister."

As the boys turned to leave, the treasurer of the beer tore one of the cans from the litter.

"Here, Mister."

Inside, Jack stoked the fire. He drew the curtains fully, this time.

"Let them at it, eh, Millie? Sure they're only young."

Slumping into the armchair, he snapped open the can, sipping its cool contents. The dog sat at his feet, staring into the flickering flames. It had been an eventful day. Jack replayed the encounter with the van in his head. It had been close. It could have been the day he and Maura were reunited. He looked at the photos on the mantle. Once-a-year grandchildren with American accents. Maura was in most of them, smiling proudly. The most recent was two years ago, when senility had robbed most of the light from her eyes. Rather like the woman in the A&E, only her light was gone for different reasons. It had taken her misfortune to awaken Jack to what his wife must have gone through. Her sister, Kathleen, was still alive, but he doubted he'd have the courage to ask her what had happened. Their father was dead. Maura was dead. What was the point now?

Before the Church scandals broke, Jack, and many like him, had never heard such a word as paedophile. A word that chilled, sounding like the Latin name for an insect. It was the worst thing a human could be. Was that what Christopher Millar had been? Maura always found an excuse not to allow the children have sleepovers at their grandparents. And Jack always found an excuse not to question why. Denial covered many a cracked wall. Now the cracks were finally ghosting through.

He felt every sinew in his body tension like guitar strings, until he crushed the can with arthritic fingers. The beer spewed from the top, dribbling onto the floor. The dog sniffed it, then turned her head.

"I'm sorry, Maura. I never saw it. Not really. When I did, I denied it…fuck it anyway."

Only one question remained now. What if he'd known? If Maura had sat him down all those years ago and told him her story, buying herself some insurance against him finding out years into the marriage and walking because he couldn't handle it.

Would he have felt any differently about her?

Jack's eyes found the picture on the wall. November `54. Faded and grainy. He, dark haired and broad shouldered. Maura, at his side, braided hair and white dress. The answer was simple, contained in that single moment, captured that morning. It was in his heart now.

She would have been no less lovely to him. She was Maura. His Maura. All the Christy Millars in the world couldn't change that.

The thunder of rockets snapped him into the present. Coloured lights filtered through the curtains. Blue, green, red. He got up and peered out the window. The sky rained bright sparks. Once, Maura would have loved it.

The fire drew him back, and he switched on the news.

More turmoil in Syria. Some people's troubles were only beginning.

End

www.ingramcontent.com/pod-product-compliance
Lightning Source LLC
Chambersburg PA
CBHW071257130626
46556CB00003B/1350